Juan José Saer was born in Santa Fé, Argentina in 1937. He became one of the leading writers of the post-Borges generation. In 1968 he moved to Paris and taught literature at the university in Rennes, Brittany. In 1988 he was awarded Spain's prestigious Nadal Prize. His work has been translated into all major languages. He died in 2005.

Praise for Juan José Saer

'Haunting and beautifully written... The author's preoccupations are reminiscent of his fellow Argentinians Borges and Cortazar but his vision is fresh and unique' *Independent on Sunday*

'Saer's novel combines elements of the haunting metaphysical ambiguity of Jorge Luis Borges' poetry and Graham Greene's sensual description of the dark corners of the physical world and the human soul. The evocative imagery and ideas revealed in *The Witness* are not easily forgotten' *Washington Times*

'Let me make myself clear: *The Witness* is a great book and the name of its author, Juan José Saer, must be added to the list of the best South American writers' *Le Monde*

'There is no magical realism, no baroque exoticism and not a particle of sentimentality that sometimes colours Latin American fiction, but instead an intensity of poetic description and meditation...Saer's luminous prose imparts awesome meaning to the word "discover"' *Times Educational Supplement*

'Shades of Melville and Conrad's *Heart of Darkness* influence an urgent narrative which unfolds through prose which has the terse

The Witness

Juan José Saer

Translated by Margaret Jull Costa

A complete catalogue record for this book can be
obtained from the British Library on request

The right of Juan José Saer to be identified as the
author of this work has been asserted in accordance with
the Copyright, Designs and Patents Act 1988

First published as *El Entenado* in 1983

First published in 1990 by Serpent's Tail,
First published in this edition in 2009 by Serpent's Tail
an imprint of Profile Books Ltd
3A Exmouth House
Pine Street
London EC1R 0JH
website: www.serpentstail.com

ISBN 978 1 84668 691 7

Printed and bound in Great Britain by CPI Bookmarque Ltd,
Croydon, Surrey

10 9 8 7 6 5 4 3 2 1

For Laurence Gueguen

The translator would like to thank Pete Ayrton, Annella McDermott, Faye Carney, Christopher Gordon Brown and Brenda Woods for their help and advice.

Further inland there is a vast tract which is uninhabited. Above this desolate region dwell the Cannibals, who are a people apart...

Herodotus, IV, 18

WHAT I REMEMBER MOST ABOUT THOSE EMPTY shores is the vastness of the sky. Standing beneath that expanse of blue, I felt how small I was; on those yellow sands we were as insignificant as ants in the middle of a desert. Now that I am an old man, I prefer to live out my days in cities because city life is bounded by horizons and because cities conceal the sky. There we used to sleep out in the open at night, almost crushed by the stars. You felt you could reach out and touch them: they were so big, so uncountable, crackling with light, with only slivers of blackness separating one from another. It was as if the sky were a volcano wall riddled with holes that let you glimpse its inner incandescence.

It was being left an orphan that drove me to the ports. The smell of the sea and damp rope, the slow, stiff sails of ships arriving and departing, the conversations of old sailors, the varied perfumes of spices, the piled-up merchandise, the prostitutes, the alcohol and the ships' captains, the noise and the bustle. All of that, as far back as I can remember, took the place of a father and mother for me: it lulled me to sleep, it was home, it gave me both shelter and education. I used to do odd jobs and run errands for whores and sailors. Occasionally I would sleep in the house of some relations but more often on sacks in warehouses. Gradually I left my childhood behind me: then one day a whore rewarded my services with my first experience of sex, and a sailor, who I had run an errand for, repaid my diligence with a swig of hard liquor. In this way, as they say, I became a man.

By that time the ports no longer sufficed: I hungered for the open sea. Children blame the intransigence of the world on their own callowness and lack of knowledge; they think that far off on the other side of the ocean, on the farther shore of experience, the fruit is more succulent, more real, the sun yellower and kinder, men's actions and words more intelligible, clear-cut and just. These beliefs – they were also, of course, a consequence of my poverty – fired me with enthusiasm and I set about finding a place as cabin boy. Where the ship was going was of little importance, what mattered was to get far away from the place I was in, to go towards another point on the curved horizon, some place of fierce delights.

Twenty years or so earlier it had been discovered that the Indies could be reached by sailing west and so they had become the fashionable destination. Ships returned from there loaded down with spices, bruised and battered, after drifting over unknown seas. People in the ports talked of little else and at times the topic fired their faces and conversations with a crazed intensity. The unknown is an abstraction; the known, a desert; but what is half-known, half-seen, is the perfect breeding ground for desire and hallucination. When the sailors talked they mixed everything up: the Chinese, the Indians, the New World, precious stones, spices, gold, greed and myth. They spoke of cities paved with gold, of paradise on earth, of sea monsters that rose suddenly out of the water; sailors, mistaking these monsters' backs for islands, would land on them and camp amongst the folds of hard, scaly skin. I listened to all these stories in amazement, my heart pounding. Since I, like all children, believed that I was destined for glory and somehow immune from disaster, my desire to set sail grew stronger with each new tale I heard, whether wonderful or terrifying. At last my chance came. A captain, one of the most experienced navigators in the kingdom, was organizing an expedition to the Molucca Islands and I managed to secure a place on it.

It was not hard. People talked a lot in the port but when it actually came to joining ship, very few came forward. Later I would understand why. Anyway, I had no difficulty at all getting the job of cabin boy on the flagship, the largest of the three ships making up the expedition. And when I arrived to sign on, it was as if they had been expecting me; they welcomed me with open arms and assured me we would have an excellent voyage and in a few months would return from the Indies laden with treasure. The captain was not there; he was busy at Court and was only due to arrive on the day we sailed. The recruiting officer assigned me a berth in the sailors' quarters and told me to report back later to be briefed about my duties. During the week before we sailed I went ashore almost every day to run errands for the officers and for the sailors too; but I never hung about the streets or taverns because, so proud was I of my job as cabin boy, I wanted to carry out my duties to perfection.

At last the day of departure arrived. The evening before, the captain, followed by the first mate and with a fair-sized retinue in tow, had arrived to inspect every nook and cranny of the ships. Once we were out at sea he called the officers and sailors up on deck and delivered a brief sermon extolling the virtues of discipline, courage and the love of God, King and hard toil. He was an austere, distant man with nothing coarse about him; sometimes he could be seen working on deck with the same vigour as the sailors. At other times he would stand alone on the bridge, his gaze fixed on the empty horizon. Fixed, it seemed, not on the sea or the sky but rather on something within himself, on some lingering, unending memory; or perhaps the emptiness of the horizon lodged inside him and held him there, unblinking, stone-still. He treated me with absent-minded kindness, as if one of us were not there. Although the crew respected him they did not fear him. His uncompromising beliefs seemed heartfelt and he applied them to the letter, but he was detached from them too. It was as if there were two captains: the one who gave out orders with mathematical precision, orders doubtless emanating from the Crown, and this other immobile figure on the bridge, staring at some invisible point between sea and sky.

Our voyage through that blue monotony lasted more than three months. Within a few days of setting sail we were in warm waters and it was then I first became aware of the limitless sky which my mind would never again be rid of. The sky was mirrored by the sea, and the ships, spaced out at regular intervals one behind the other, seemed to be slowly crossing a vast blue sphere that turned black at night, its vault studded with points of light. Not a fish, bird or cloud did we see. We held the whole of the known world in our memories. We were its only guarantors in that totally smooth, blue universe. Day after day, the sun, red on the horizon, yellow and incandescent at its zenith, bore witness to the fact that something other than just sky existed. But it was of little consolation. After several weeks we were seized by delirium: beliefs, reduced to mere memory, proved too fragile a foundation. Sea and sky began to lose their names, their meanings. As the ropes, the wooden hull of the ship and its sails grew rougher to the touch and the bodies strolling the deck became more solid, so their real existence became progressively more problematic. At times it seemed we were not moving forward at all. The three ships strung out in a ragged line, some distance one from the other, seemed transfixed in blue space. The colour was not entirely unvarying: it changed, for example, when the sun appeared on the horizon behind us and when it sank below it again beyond the ships' motionless bows. The captain stood contemplating those changes from his position on the bridge, as if bewitched. At times we almost longed for a sighting of one of those sea monsters so talked about in ports. But no monster appeared.

In this strange situation further vicissitudes await the cabin boy. The complete absence of women has the effect of emphasizing the ambivalence of his still adolescent features. As the voyage progresses, things which in port would seem repugnant to the sailors (decent family men every one of them) come to be seen as quite natural, just as, once fallen on hard times, the ardent defender of private property finds his firm principles gnawed by hunger and soon cannot look at a neighbour's chicken without imagining it plucked and roasted. It has to be said, too, that delicacy was not a strong point amongst the sailors. More often than not their idea of a declaration of love was a knife held to the throat. I had no option but to choose between my honour and my life. More than once I was on the point of complaining to the captain but my suitors' earnest threats dissuaded me. At last I opted for sly consent, seeking out the protection of the strongest amongst them to turn the situation to my advantage. My dealings with the women of the port proved in the end useful. By watching them I had realized with a child's intuition that selling themselves was just a means of survival and that in their way of life honour came a poor second to strategy. Questions of personal taste were also superfluous. The fundamental vice of all human beings is the desire to stay alive and in good health no matter what, to make real our images of hope whatever the cost. In my case what I wanted more than anything else was to reach those paradise islands: so I let myself be passed from hand to hand, and I must confess that now and then, in my role as beardless and still ambivalent adolescent, I derived some pleasure from my dealings with the sailors, who, to an orphan like myself, had something of the father about them. We were still engaged in these comings and goings when we sighted land.

We were overjoyed. These unknown shores were proof at last of the world's diversity. The palm-edged yellow sands, deserted in the noonday sun, helped us to forget the long, monotonous, uneventful voyage from which we emerged as if from a period of madness. Our enthusiastic cries were a welcome to the contingency. We were passing from utter monotony into the multiplicity of the possible. Before our eyes the smooth sea was turning into dry sand, into trees that were the start of a rugged landscape that began at the water's edge, a landscape of ravines, hills and jungle; there were birds, beasts and every kind of animal, vegetable and mineral offered by a superabundant earth. Before us was firm ground onto which we could anchor our delirium. The captain, observing us from the bridge as if all this were no concern of his, did not, however, share our enthusiasm. Smiling a distant, thoughtful smile, apparent more in his eyes than on his lips, he contemplated the crew and the landscape without actually taking them in. The expression on his heavily bearded face deepened the lines around his eyes. As we approached the shore the crew's euphoria intensified. Here was an end to all suffering and uncertainty; that gentle, terrestrial place seemed to us benign but, more than that, real. The captain gave orders to drop anchor and make ready the boats to take us ashore. Many of the sailors and even some of the officers did not wait for the boats: they dived into the water from the gunwale and swam to the shore ahead of the boats. As we approached they gestured to us, jumping up and down on the beach half-naked, waving their arms, dripping water, happy to be on solid ground at last.

When we arrived we scattered like stampeding animals. Some just ran aimlessly off in all directions; others ran round tracing a tight circle on the sand while others again jumped up and down on the spot. One group lit a huge bonfire, its flames pale in the midday sun, and stood transfixed by it. Two old sailors, standing by a tree, were teasing a large bird that could not decide whether or not to flee and instead leapt screeching from bough to bough. Behind them, inland, at the foot of a small hill, several men were chasing birds that looked like chickens with multicoloured plumage. Some men climbed trees, others scratched around in the earth. One man, standing on the shore, was urinating into the sea. Incomprehensibly, some of the sailors had preferred to stay on the ship and, leaning over the rail, watched us from afar. Dusk found us all on the beach grouped around the fire on which were cooking the spoils of our hunting and fishing; as night fell, the flames lit up the bearded, sweating faces of the sailors seated in a circle. One of them, an old man, began to sing. The rest of us kept time with our hands. Then, slowly, as the fire died down, tiredness got the better of us. Some men were already nodding where they sat, others lay down on their sides on the warm sand, others again sought out a place that would be sheltered from the dew, at the foot of the hill or beneath a tree. Ten or twelve men took a boat and went back to the ships to sleep. Silence descended on the beach. Under cover of the dark, and just as a joke, one sailor let out a prolonged fart which was greeted with roars of laughter. I stretched out on my back to look at the stars. With no moon in view the sky was teeming with them, yellow, red, and green: some glittered brightly, others sparkled or shone hard and steady. From time to time, a single star would slide off into the blackness tracing an arc of light. The stars were so close I felt I could have touched them. I had heard an officer say that each star was a world, inhabited like our own, and that our earth was round and floated in space just like a star. If, seen from the beach, those stars inhabited by men like us appeared no more than tiny points of light, I shuddered to think what our real size must be.

The next day I was woken by the sound of raised voices. Officers and sailors, some standing, some crouching, were arguing on the beach. They were spread out over the sands and spoke in loud but controlled voices, as if reining in their anger. The sun tinged the sea red and made the shapes of the boats silhouetted against its first rays even blacker. An order had come from the main ship to weigh anchor at once and set course for the south. The lands we had found were not the Indies but some unknown place. We were to tack along these shores and sail on to the Indies which lay beyond them. There were two opposing groups in the argument. The first, the majority, bowed to the orders of the captain. The second, comprising two officers and fifteen or so sailors, were of the view that we should remain in the land we had discovered and begin its exploration. They were locked in this battle of wills for nearly an hour. As tempers grew more heated, hands, as if by instinct, were quick to reach for swordhilts. Every now and then their barely controlled voices would let out an insult or an exclamation. When the first group was talking, those in the second group would shake their heads, rejecting what was said from the outset, not even deigning to listen to the others' arguments. When it was the second group's turn to speak, the members of the first group just looked at one another and smiled disdainfully, adopting a superior air. At one point, the rebels, three or four of whom were sitting on the sand, got up, drew their swords and took a step back. Without advancing, those in the other group also made ready their weapons. The sun glinted on the bronze and steel. The metal helmets gleamed fleetingly with each angry movement the men made. But after that initial show of bluster, the two groups stood still, several paces apart, swords in hand, staring at one another. The long, lean morning shadows of those wishing to follow orders stretched out across the sand, their pointed heads breaking between the legs of their adversaries. Battle seemed imminent when one of the rebels, whose group was facing the sea, sheathed his sword, cried out: 'The captain!' and began distractedly but hastily to brush the sand from the seat of his trousers and the rest of his clothes.

Calm and dignified, the captain was standing stock-still in the boat amongst the rowers, his feet braced against the sides, his right hand resting on the hilt of the sword that hung at his left side. If his body swayed at all it was to the pitch of the boat, as if his feet were nailed fast to its floor. That they were not became clear as soon as the boat reached the shore and the captain, erect and agile, stepped over the heads of the rowers and on to dry land and, without a moment's hesitation, advanced resolutely up the beach. His boots, weapons, jewels and doubloons set up a repetitive, metallic rhythm as he walked. His long shadow preceded him, gliding over the yellow sands. Those of us who were on the beach watching his approach assumed he would deliver one of his absent-minded harangues as soon as he reached us. However, when he did reach us, he confounded us all by continuing on past without breaking step. Then we realized that his steady, dignified gaze, which had appeared to be focused on us from the moment the boat left the ship, was in fact fixed on the trees at the foot of the hill where the beach ended and the jungle began. He was so intent on this point that when we saw that he was going to walk straight past, many of us, out of curiosity and surprise, turned our heads in the same direction; but however hard we scrutinized and peered at the point in question, we could see nothing unusual, only the green fringe of vegetation and the green, gentle slope of the hill that marked the edge of the jungle. With solemn, measured step, the captain continued walking for some distance yet until at last, brusquely and without changing direction, he stopped and stood where he was, absolutely still. At first I had thought – as doubtless had many of the others on the beach – that the captain must have been putting the final touches to his speech as he approached, rounding out the phrases he intended to address to us and the ideas he wished to communicate; I had thought his only aim in passing us by was to polish the speech that would be delivered once he had gone as far as he could on the beach and had spun elegantly round on his heels to return whence he had come. However, against all our expectations, he did neither of these things. Instead he remained with his back to us, as still as a statue, gazing, no doubt unblinkingly, at that same uncertain point somewhere amongst the trees at the edge of the jungle. He remained like that for a good five minutes. The men on the beach, rebels and loyalists alike, completely forgot the argument they had been embroiled in until only a few moments before and, after a while, began to exchange questioning looks. Just a few yards away the captain's back remained firm and erect. My gaze drifted from him to the two groups of sailors separated by a patch of empty sand with the long shadows of those nearest the shore stretching across it, to the impassive rowers waiting in the boat and, beyond them, to the three ships whose sails were beginning to gleam in the morning light. There was not a breath of wind and, though the sun had only just risen, it was already starting to blaze down on the deserted beach. There was no sound to be heard either, apart from one too monotonous and familiar for us to pay it any heed, that of the waves breaking on the beach in semicircles of white foam, rocking the boat and the rowers in its regular rhythm. Expectation united the sailors who stood immobilized by the same shared sense of stupefaction. At last, after the almost unbearable waiting, something happened: the captain, still with his back turned to us, let out a long, deep, heartfelt sigh that could be clearly heard in the silent morning and that sent a slight tremor through his solid, upright frame. Some sixty years have passed since that morning yet I can say without the slightest exaggeration that something about the depth of that long-drawn-out sigh so impressed me that it will remain with me till I die. The effect on the sailors, however, was to replace the look of amazement on their faces with the beginnings of panic. The most incredible of monsters inhabiting that unknown land would have been greeted with less horror than that melancholy sigh. Immediately afterwards, however, the captain finally span round on his heels and began to walk back the way he had come, passing the sailors without even registering their presence and shaking his head, his short beard buried in his chest, as he made his way back towards the rowing boat. Once on board, he again stepped over the heads of the sailors and then stood unmoving amongst them as they began to row. With slow pulls the boat moved away from the shore to the ships at anchor. The sailors said nothing, forgot their differences and sheathed their swords. Then, without speaking or even daring to look one another in the eye, they started walking towards the empty boats bobbing in the waves at the other end of the beach.

The ships headed south, always keeping within sight of land. At times the coast, which we kept constantly in view, would withdraw a little, bend to form a semi-circular bay or push jagged rocks out into the water, forcing us further out to sea. Sometimes we spied beasts and birds, or long-haired quadrupeds browsing on the shore, or monkeys swinging with impudent agility from tree to tree, or multicoloured birds darting about the ships' bows only to abruptly change direction and disappear back into the jungle. Of people we saw not a sign. No one. If these were the Indies as was claimed, there was no evidence of any Indian inhabitants, no self-aware beings like ourselves within whom might burn the small flame that gives shape, colour and volume to the space around and lends it its externality.

The captain, who before had been merely distant, now became remote: he seemed to float in some inaccessible dimension. In the days following our disembarkation, he was scarcely seen on deck. His subordinates took care of everything and he did not leave his cabin. At first we thought he must be ill, but the sight of his robust frame on the two or three brief, absent-minded appearances he put in convinced us otherwise. One night they sent me from the kitchen to serve him his meal because the sailor who usually did so was ill. When I returned to clear the table I knocked on the cabin door and, receiving no reply and thinking he must have gone out, I decided to go in. Then I saw that he was in fact still sitting at the table, alone in the middle of the brightly lit cabin, carefully studying the fish I had served him some time ago and which lay untouched on his plate. He did not even hear me come in, or at any rate nothing in his attitude indicated that he had. The captain's gaze, simultaneously intense and vague, remained fixed on the fish and, in particular, on the one round eye that had remained intact during cooking; though lifeless, it seemed to exercise an inordinate fascination over him, to attract and hold his attention like a spinning red spiral.

As we sailed along the coast, we entered a sea of fresh, brown waters. It was calm and desolate. As we neared the shore we could see that the landscape had changed and that the terrain was becoming less hilly and more austere. Only the heat was constant, unmitigated by that strange-coloured sea, so unlike the other blue sea which cools the beaches of the world with winds that blow in from the deep. We saw nothing but blue sky, smooth golden-brown waters and empty shores as we entered the 'sweet' sea: this was what the captain named it when we landed, invoking the King with his customary mechanical gestures. From the shore we watched him plunge almost waist-deep into the water, scything the air and skimming the waves with his sword in ceremonial gestures. My inexperienced eyes followed the captain's precise, complicated gestures with interest but failed to perceive the change my imagination anticipated. After its baptism and appropriation the dumb earth stubbornly withheld any sign or signal. From the boat, as we moved off towards what we took to be the mouth of the river that gave the sea its brown colour, I remained staring at the spot where we had disembarked; although only a few minutes had passed since we left, I could find no trace of our presence there. It was once again empty coast, blue sky and golden-brown water. We nursed the illusion that by discovering this unknown land we were laying claim to it, as if before us there had been nothing but an immanent void which our presence peopled with a corporeal landscape. But when we left it, in that state of hallucinatory somnolence brought on by the monotony of the trip, we saw all too clearly that the space we considered ourselves the founders of had always in fact been there and had allowed our passage through it with indifference, retaining no trace of our passing and even swallowing up any signs we had left behind for those who came after us. Each time we disembarked we were like a fleeting irritation come from nowhere, an ephemeral fever that glimmered for a moment at the edge of the water and then was gone. We sailed on for a few leagues after entering the estuary of the wild river – of which I later realized there was more than one – startling the parrots nesting in the red earth of the banks and barely rousing the slow-moving clumps of alligators on the muddy shores. The smell of those rivers is like no other on earth. It is the smell of primeval beginnings, the dank smell of things painfully taking shape, caught in the very process of growing. Leaving behind the monotonous sea and travelling down those rivers was like descending from limbo on to earth. We could almost see life being remade out of the putrefying mosses, the vegetable mulch that rocked in its bosom thousands of tiny, blind, formless creatures. The absence of human life only reinforced the illusion of life newborn. We travelled like this for almost a whole day until at last, at nightfall, we came to a halt between those primordial shores. The captain prudently postponed disembarking until the following morning, for fear of wild beasts, or men, or other unnamed terrors.

Though many years have passed since then, the memory of that day still evokes for me the essential flavour of dawn: the voices a little hoarse from sleep, the first early-morning noises creating a well of sound in the dark, and one's own being rising up from the depths, reconciling itself to the coming day, after being rudely shaken awake by the hand of someone already up and about in the innocent morning. On that occasion it was a lugubrious old-timer who woke me. I was to form part of a group to go ashore with the captain on a reconnaissance. Half-asleep and still pulling on our clothes we gathered on deck where the captain was waiting for us, wrapped in the blue penumbra of dawn. The morning star, brilliant and unmoving, hung above the ropes and masts silhouetted against that penumbra. There were eleven of us, including the captain. We took one boat and headed for the western shore. I can still remember seeing behind us, as we rowed away from the ships, the red blur staining the sky beyond the trees on the opposite shore. It was almost daylight when we reached land. Our presence on the shore threw the birds into still greater uproar. We walked ahead bathed in the morning light. The captain had completely laid aside his authoritarian manner, adopting instead our wonder and caution, though with no show of humility. Freeing his mind from the rigidity of command seemed to leave him in a state of animal readiness that would make him better able to confront whatever these unknown lands might hold in store for us. After casting a long, dazed look about us we pressed on, leaving the boat bobbing on the river. In some places the undergrowth was taller than we were, in others it barely reached our waists; sometimes we would cross small woods of stunted trees whose branches were filled with flowering creepers and singing birds. At last we emerged into a bare, deserted field, yellowed and scorched no doubt by the intense heat. Though the high sun lit up everything, it still somehow failed to make the world before us seem any more immediate or present. By mid-morning the ships anchored behind us on a now imagined river were only an improbable memory. For a few minutes we stood transfixed, contemplating as one man the same landscape, not knowing whether other eyes had ever scanned it or whether, when we turned around, it might not simply disappear behind our backs, the illusion of a moment. We had been walking now for two or three hours; as it would take the same time to retrace our steps we turned round and started going back the way we had come, sweating and silent with the sun before us. Our state of mind and this land were one and the same thing; it was impossible to imagine one without the other. If we really were the only human presence since the beginning of time to have pushed through that parched vegetation, it was as difficult to imagine it continuing to exist in our absence exactly as we saw, smelled and heard it, as it was to imagine that barren landscape ever ceasing to be present in our minds. The solitary sun burned in a sky of such an intense blue that its surface seemed troubled by waves of turbulent, changing colour, like fragments of fire licking round a scorched dry centre. The captain seemed utterly terrified – if one can use that word to describe the state of mind of a man possessed of unbearable knowledge from which nevertheless all fear is absent. The few words he uttered came out in a weak, broken, almost grief-stricken voice; the sweat running down his forehead and cheeks into the dense black scrub of his beard left damp, muddy trails around his eyes that immediately made one think of tears. Now that I am an old man and many years have passed since that shining morning, I can begin to understand that what lay behind the captain's feelings in that precise moment was the realization that all his life he had been mistaken about the kind of man he was. In that empty morning, his very being was laid bare as no doubt (within the capabilities of its limited understanding) is the soul of the hare when in the corner of some field it encounters the hunter's trap.

As I recall, we reached the coast about midday. The sun blazed down on the ships and the water; the searing light imposed an absolute stillness on everything, emphasizing the stark, problematic essence of all the physical objects trapped in its burning arena Panting and sweating, we came to a halt on the damp clay, emerging suddenly from the undergrowth into the view of the men watching for us from the ships. Disappointed perhaps that the expedition had proved so uneventful, the captain seemed undecided about what to do and delayed our embarkation, gazing slowly about in all directions and responding distractedly and in monosyllables to any remarks from his sailors. When we were almost at the water's edge, he turned round, retreated a few yards, then began to shake his head like someone about to put forward, in the face of overwhelming evidence to the contrary, some deeply held belief All this while his eyes were constantly scanning the undergrowth, the trees, the ground and the water. We stood round him, not knowing what to do, waiting. Finally, looking at us with that same expression of mingled belief and distrust, he began: 'This is a land without . . .' at the same time raising his arm and shaking his fist, trying perhaps with that gesture to reinforce the truth of the statement he was about to deliver. 'This is a land without . . .': those were the captain's precise words when an arrow shot out from the undergrowth that rose up behind him and pierced his throat, so suddenly and unexpectedly that he remained standing there with his eyes still open, frozen for a few moments with his arm raised in that affirmatory gesture, before falling to the ground. For a fraction of a second the only thing I registered was my astonished realization that apart from me everyone in the captain's party was lying absolutely still on the ground; they had been pierced in various parts of their bodies, but most often through the throat and chest, by arrows that seemed to have come out of nowhere to embed themselves with awful accuracy in my companions' unsuspecting flesh. I had just been witness to an event which would be the talk of the kingdom, possibly of all Europe, yet I was unable at that moment to tremble at its horrific significance or even to grasp what was going on or what had just occurred. All I remember of that moment (for what came afterwards happened very fast) is the sense of strangeness that overwhelmed me. In a few seconds my extraordinary situation became crystal clear: with the deaths of the men taking part in the expedition, all certainty of a common experience was gone and I was left all alone in the world with the difficulties that that implied. This state did not last long. A horde of naked dark-skinned men emerged from the undergrowth, brandishing bows and arrows. While one group busied themselves gathering up the bodies, the others crowded round me pointing, touching me with a gentle enthusiasm that provoked peals of contented, admiring laughter, and repeating again and again the same two shrill, rapid sounds: *Def-ghi! Def-ghi! Def-ghi!* Again that lasted only a short time. My sense of floating, of being somewhere else, was much more powerful than any feeling of terror. And before I knew it, before I could turn my head to glance back towards the ships which, unless I am mistaken, must still have been there in the middle of the river, these same naked, dark-skinned men had collected up the dead bodies and were running nimbly and effortlessly towards the undergrowth, forcing me to keep pace with them for a good hour. Each of the two strong men who flanked me kept a firm but gentle grip on one of my arms, guiding me deftly over the rugged terrain, never once addressing me by word or look. They seemed to know by heart every tree, path and thicket. When they stopped by the side of a quiet stream in the shade of some trees they were not even out of breath. Seeing another section of that alien land whilst at rest was no less strange or remarkable to me than it had been passing through an unknown landscape blurred by the inevitable jogging up and down of constant running; this had had the effect of making everything I saw around me tremble as if in a constant state of flux: shifting up and down and from side to side, as if the whole landscape were made up of identical layers clumsily superimposed. While under the trees that grew by the edge of the stream one group of Indians stood deep in discussion, accompanying their words with many ponderous gestures, I threw myself down on the ground breathing fast, listening to my heart pounding in my breast. It appeared that the men under the trees were talking about me, for every now and then they would stare over at me as if weighing my fate. I still marvel at my lack of fear. Not for a moment did it occur to me that I would share the same fate as the captain and my other companions; time would prove me right. It is true that the singularity of my situation, in many respects analogous to those we encounter in our dreams, made me perceive events as if from far off and as if they were happening to someone else, just as one listens to someone else's adventures or in dreams passes unmoved through the most terrible dangers. Thus that cluster of naked men and the piles of dead bodies before me were like some remote image that bore no relation to my own reality nor to anything which until that moment I had thought of as an experience of mine. When I had recovered a little from my fatigue, I sat up and looked around As always when my mind empties, I began mechanically to count: occasionally I grew confused since they were all naked and looked rather alike to me and some moved restlessly about: going to the river's edge, approaching the group in discussion, walking over to look at the bodies of the captain and my companions, coming up to me to observe me for a few minutes with polite attention. After several recounts, and using various methods of verification, I concluded that there were ninety-four of them. The next day I counted again and arrived at the same result. They were all male and neither very young nor very old. There were no more than twenty of them involved in the discussion under the trees. The others merely came and went.

Another reason for my strange calm was the consistent courtesy with which the savages approached me, touched me (usually with the tips of outstretched fingers) and spoke to me. There was one word, divided into two separate, easily identifiable sounds, that they used when addressing me or referring to my person. When they repeated that word in their shrill voices – *Def-ghi, Def-ghi. Def-ghi* – they usually accompanied it with musical laughter or loud guffaws, smiling at me and tenderly touching my shoulders, arms or chest, or made incidental remarks of which I was clearly the object, judging by the dark fingers pointed insistently in my direction. Sometimes one of the men would crouch in front of me and stare at me with a dream-like persistence. Some brought water and fruit, which, after overcoming my initial distrust, I ended up devouring. With exaggeratedly courteous gestures, others invited me to sit down in the shade of the trees near the meeting, for the two Indians who had been at my side throughout the run had left me sitting in the full blaze of the afternoon sun. When I understood the invitation and moved towards the trees, one of the Indians cut off a branch and started sweeping the ground so that it would be clean for me to sit down.

The discussion beneath the trees lasted several hours: at times the speakers grew lethargic, seeming to lose the thread of their perorations, even dropping off to sleep in the middle of them, only to resume them again much later, satisfying the general mood of expectancy that showed no signs of diminishing during the long silences. Indeed such lethargy seemed to fill the orators with enthusiasm and sharpen the attention of their motionless companions. The group finally ended their discussions as the sun was beginning to set, before it had sunk completely below the horizon and still gave out a thin green-yellow light. Two or three started shouting orders to gather together the scattered men while the others again began loading up the bodies and, once I had been rejoined on either side by the Indians who had escorted me before, we recommenced our run.

The Indians' deferential attitude towards me was again evident during the next stage of the journey. Gently and wordlessly the two on either side of me

grasped me by my elbows and lifted me up a few inches
so that my feet did not touch the ground, thus saving me
the effort of actually running. At first I did not quite see
what they were trying to do and started kicking, but
when I understood their intentions I made myself rigid,
with forearms a little raised, fingers drawn in, useless
legs gripped together, and arms held a little away from
my body so that my elbows rested effortlessly, and in a
way naturally, on the firm, supporting hands. Such was
the skill of these men that at times I felt no reverberation
at all from their bare feet thudding on the ground, so
that my vision was not blurred and the landscape on
either side of me slid by as placidly as if I were moving
over the smoothest of surfaces. When the bumps began
again I would feel them adjusting their strong grip on my
elbows, trying as far as possible to avoid my being
disturbed by the jolting, which incidentally seemed to
have little effect on their own comfort. The run lasted
the rest of the day, without pause. To be honest it was
more of a gentle trot, a rhythm the column of men
seemed accustomed to and from which no one departed.
It was a regular, restful trotting that after some hours
became so monotonous that by dusk I had fallen asleep. I
was woken by a luminous white blur like a fixed flame
swaying in front of me; only after some time did I
recognize it as the moon. In the darkness my carriers
were breathing easily, almost inaudibly. The bare feet of
ninety-four men again and again striking the ground
produced no more than a slight scrunching noise that
was lost almost immediately in the dark. Then dawn
broke and the huge moon disappeared below the horizon;
daybreak came at once, followed by sunrise and then
morning. The sun, rising behind us, remained fixed for a
moment over our heads and then began to decline,

slowly, before our eyes, until its light again grew tenuous, taking on that same green-yellow hue. Then, high up on the bank of a vast river of golden-brown waters, we stopped. The river was wide enough to accommodate several flat islands which broke its flow in midstream. The late sun danced on the water. My two escorts released me and I felt the ground beneath my feet again. Something in my head, and everything around me with it, was spinning and swinging, and I had to sit down before I collapsed. If its rivers were anything to go by that land must have been infinite or at least that was the almost dizzying impression that the proud river gave.

The terrain we had crossed had been rather high, softly undulating and criss-crossed by quiet streams which now and then were shallow enough to allow us to ford them. What land I could glimpse from the bank above the wild river and the squat islands, seemed flat and with no visible hills; it was an earth-green plain that stretched uninterrupted as far as the horizon, with only the sky as contrast. I dragged myself to the edge of the bank and stayed there a while observing the landscape and the men. They were lying down, seemingly to catch their breath, or walking along the narrow shores of the river where it lapped the bank. That was when I counted them again: there were ninety-four. Only a day after having seen them for the first time, I was so used to them that the captain, my companions and the ships all seemed to me like the unconnected fragments of an ill-remembered dream. I think that was the first time – aged all of fifteen – that an idea with which I am now familiar first occurred to me: namely that the memory of an event is not sufficient proof that it really happened, just as the memory of a dream that we believe we had in the past, many years or months before the moment in which we remember it, is not sufficient proof that the dream took place in the distant past rather than the night before the day on which we recall it, or even that it occurred before the precise moment we state that it has occurred. For me, despite the physical fact of their bodies piled up at the foot of the river bank, by the edge of the water, the captain and my companions had already disappeared for ever from my life. Up until that moment I had had no time to feel compassion for them – or for myself either. I felt light, almost as if I did not exist at all, and events, however tenuous and fleeting, now picked me up and carried me with them as my strong, impassive escorts had done before.

We did not stop for long. It was as if the resting period were only for my benefit or were just a formality. The Indians had hidden a multitude of craft made from hollowed-out treetrunks amongst the foliage that grew on the steep slope of the bank. These they pushed quickly into the water, distributing themselves and the bodies amongst them. The men always seemed to move with lightning speed: in one day they had slain the captain and the rest of my companions, run many miles with only the briefest of rests; and now they pushed the canoes out into the water (something they also did at a run), and immediately jumped in and started paddling with steady, vigorous strokes that carried us forward into the reddening dusk reflected in the water. In crossing the river they gave me further signs of their deference: I had a canoe to myself, paddled, inevitably, by my two impassive but energetic escorts.

The river I was crossing for the first time, which would form my horizon and be my home for ten years, flows down from the north, from the jungle, out into the sea the poor captain had called the sweet sea. The Indians

call it the father of rivers. And it is true that, as it flows
on down, it does in fact engender rivers, rivers which
multiply as they near the estuary and break off at a
certain point from the main riverbed, rivers which in
turn engender other rivers, in a tendency to infinite
multiplication which the banks, eroded by the waters,
can barely contain. It is a river of many shores formed by
its sombre, marshy islands. The men who live nearby are
the same colour as that muddy shore, as if they too had
been engendered by the river. This fact caused Father
Quesada to remark years later, when he heard my
descriptions of the Indians, that I had lived close to
paradise for ten years and had never known it; that the
flesh of those men still bore traces of the mud out of
which the first man was formed; and that they were
without a doubt the unacknowledged offspring of Adam.

Dodging and skirting the islands, we approached the
opposite shore whose quiet trees stood clearly outlined
in the dusk. During the crossing the rhythmic splashing
of our paddles cutting through the water seemed to me
like the inverted echo of that made by the other paddles
of the craft, with ours the nearer sound. Although not a
living soul was in sight yet, I could sense the presence of
people nearby on the coast which we were rapidly
approaching. The sight of fires scattered amongst the
trees confirmed this. But, since it was almost nightfall, it
was not until we actually reached the shore that I could
make out the dark crowd gathering on the beach: men,
women, children and old people leaving their fires that
burned beyond the trees and coming down to greet us on
the empty shore. I perceived their presence by the shine
of their dark skin, their endless chatter and, later, when
I landed, by the gentle, dignified way they touched me.
My two guards removed me from that contact after a

few minutes and, gripping me once more by the elbows,
hurried me towards the area behind the trees where the
fires were burning. Every now and then, as I was
marched away, I heard surfacing from amongst the shrill
and rapid chatter that continued behind my back the one
word which I knew referred to me – *Def-ghi, Def-ghi,
Def-ghi* – spoken with different intonation and by
different people, in the midst of the longer and shorter
sounds which formed the phrases they exchanged with
one another Led by the two Indians, I walked through
the trees to the fires burning in open areas between an
irregularly spaced but fairly extensive group of huts.
Three old women were talking peaceably round a fire,
their backs against the outside wall of one of the huts.
When they saw us coming they broke off their conversation and, with a nod in my direction, one addressed
herself rather morosely to my guards. With a facial
expression and a gesture consisting of the bunched
fingertips of one hand held towards her open mouth, she
mimed the act of eating. One of my companions replied
peremptorily: *Def-ghi, Def-ghi*. When they heard this the
old women opened their eyes inordinately wide in
pleased surprise and, shaking their heads, smiled the
same sweet, deferential smile with which all the members
of the tribe generally greeted me. Going round behind
the building outside which the old ladies were talking,
my escorts led me into one of the other huts.

Every life is a well of loneliness that only grows deeper
with the passing years. Being an orphan, I am more
conscious than most of coming from nothing and grew
up wary of the illusion of companionship which the
family offers. But that night my already great sense of
solitude suddenly became immense, as if the bottom of
that gradually deepening well had suddenly given way

and plunged me into blackness. I lay down on the ground and cried inconsolably. Writing now, with the scratching of this pen and the creaking of my chair the only clear sounds in the night, my life sustained by my quiet, almost inaudible breathing, I see my hand, the wrinkled hand of an old man, moving from left to right, leaving a black trail in the lamplight. And I realize, regardless of whether this is a memory of a real event, or just an instantaneous image without past or future freshly shaped from some mild delirium, that the crying child lost in a strange world is unknowingly witnessing his own birth. We never know when we might be born; the idea that we are born when delivered from our mothers is pure convention. Many die without ever being born; some are born, but only just, others badly, like aborted babies. Some pass from one life to another through a succession of births and, if death did not come to interrupt them, would be capable, through endless rebirths, of running the gamut of all possible worlds, as if possessed of an inexhaustible talent for innocence and abandon. Though unaware at the time, I was a foundling and, like a dazed and bloody babe leaving the dark night of his mother's womb, all I could do was cry. From beyond the trees the sound of shrill, rapid voices and the uterine smell of that vast river kept drifting up to me, until at last I fell asleep.

I was woken by the touch of something warm I had lain down on my back, my head towards the opening and my feet towards the inside of the hut: the morning sun was falling full on my face. For a long time I lay there, trying to reconstruct reality to see if I actually was awake, and at last I sat up. The fires I had seen the night before had gone out and the sun was high. It was a summer's morning with birds singing and dew on the ground. On the damp grass the morning light fragmented into drops of different colours which, when I moved my head, gleamed, tiny and intense. The various sounds from the settlement echoed up to the deep, uniformly blue sky and hung in the air. Beyond the trees I could see people working but before setting off in their direction I stood still for a moment near the pile of ash that had been last night's fire and looked around me. The scattered, fragile settlement seemed to extend quite a long way inland, for from where I was standing I could glimpse adobe walls and straw roofs scattered in no apparent order amongst the trees. Apart from the noises coming from the shore no other human sound broke the calm silence of the morning. The sunlight seeped through the thick foliage of the trees and filtered through their leaves, printing serene patterns of light on the ground or the wall of some hut. When I began walking towards the shore, a man, completely naked, who was crossing through the trees in the opposite direction and whose hands and forearms were covered in blood up to and above the elbows, stopped a moment when he saw me and began talking in his incomprehensible language. He spoke as naturally as the sailors did when they used to exchange commonplaces with me whenever we would meet on deck. When he saw that I understood little or nothing of what he was saying, he gave an embarrassed smile and went on up to the huts. I continued walking through the trees, sure that I was amongst hospitable people and allowing myself to succumb a little to the calm perfection of the morning. But when I left the trees behind me and emerged into a clearing beyond which shone the river I saw at once, and in unexpected form, the source of the noises I had heard from the moment I opened my eyes.

Working with what appeared to be their customary
rapidity and precision, the early risers of the tribe, some
fifteen naked men in two groups, were engaged on two
quite different tasks. Using sticks and branches, the first
group were making implements which, just by observing
the work of the men in the second group, I could see were
three enormous grills. Equipped with small knives
apparently made out of bone, the men of the second
group (to which the bloody but affable Indian who had
passed me under the trees doubtless belonged) were
decapitating with undeniable skill the now naked bodies
of my companions which lay on a bed of green leaves
scattered on the ground. Four of the neatly ordered
bodies, whose heads were still intact, seemed to be
looking up with great interest at the blue sky. One head
was at that moment being parted for ever by the little
bone knife from the body it had crowned for years.
Meanwhile the other five heads, which had already been
removed, were also lined up on the carpet of fresh leaves,
as if resting on their own beards. Two of the Indians,
armed with knives and rudimentary but efficient axes,
were already at work on one of the decapitated bodies,
slicing it open from the lower abdomen to the throat. No
doubt alerted by my look of intent, silent amazement,
the Indian who was in the process of beheading one of
the bodies stopped what he was doing for a moment and,
giving me a delightfully frank and friendly smile, waved
the hand wielding the knife, exclaimed *Def-ghi, Def-ghi,*
and pointed at the body. When I looked more closely I
recognized the oddly absent air of this naked body whose
head was in the process of being hacked off: it was the
captain. To make his job easier the executioner was
cradling the captain's head on his knees, so that it lay like
that of a child going to sleep in its mother's lap. The

expression on my face obviously struck them as ridiculous, for as the Indian who was busy butchering the first corpse plunged his knife into its bloody chest, he made some remark which caused those who heard it to burst out laughing. Only then did I fully take in what was happening in front of me, and I span round and ran.

I raced blindly away from the beach and the huts and off through the trees alongside the river, running until I was breathless, panting so hard that at last I had to stop. I leaned against a tree, then in a daze of exhaustion and anger, lay down for a moment on the ground until I grew calmer. Lying on my back I could see the tops of the trees with their upper leaves shining in the sun, which was already high by then. Looking up through the still leaves, I could just glimpse scraps of sky. I thought to myself: what is happening to me is my life. This is my life and this is happening to me. The indifferent way the Indians had watched me run off showed that it had not even occurred to them that I might try to escape. Where would I hide in that silent, desert land? Everything seemed so unfamiliar, so strange. I was startled from these thoughts by the sound of children's voices nearby. Slowly I sat up and, keeping very still, turned my head intently in their direction. Then I crawled noiselessly forward through the undergrowth until I spotted them near the water's edge.

There were about twenty children, boys and girls; the oldest of them could not have been more than ten and the youngest not less than three or four. They were all completely naked and were playing, healthy and happy, on the river bank. The game they were playing was both simple and strange: first they all stood in a line parallel to the river, one behind the other, and then one by one they would fall to the ground, where they lay completely still,

as if dead or asleep When the last in the line had fallen,
the others would jump to their feet, run to stand behind
the last child as he was getting up and the game would
start again. Later the line became a circle but, unlike any
of the circle games I had seen in my childhood, the
children did not face in toward the centre, but stood one
behind the other, resting their hands on the shoulders of
the child in front, so that the circle closed when the first
child in the line placed his hands on the shoulders of the
last. Sometimes the line would advance some distance
straight ahead without anyone falling to the ground.
Then, when they reached a certain point, the children
would disperse, clapping their hands, laughing and
arguing amongst themselves, as if one part of the game
had ended and they were taking a short rest before
beginning again At other times they would adopt a more
complicated configuration, a shape which I only realized
was a spiral when they began to spin. They spent a long
time making and unmaking those figures, breaking up
every now and then amid general hilarity and exuberant
shouting, until at last they dropped down on the grass by
the river and rested, breathless and quiet. After a
moment, one of them, who could not have been more
than seven years old, stood up and moved a little away
from the group for a few moments to reflect or collect his
thoughts, before drawing near again, changing his
gestures and way of walking, as if pretending to be
someone they all knew: the others greeted him with
laughter and shouts that seemed to encourage him, since
his gestures and parodic walk became more and more
exaggerated until at one point he began to utter phrases
or words which his companions celebrated with shakes
of the head or shouts which from where I lay watching I
could only just hear In the end either the little actor

grew tired or his audience's enthusiasm waned, for he then sat down again on the ground and they all became quiet and serious as they rested. Finally they got up and, skirting the water, disappeared in the direction of the settlement through the undergrowth and trees. I stayed on for some minutes contemplating the empty space where they had been, as if their noisy presence had left behind something impalpable but benevolent, something that would awake in whoever might perceive it not just joy but also compassion towards some unknown threat that was common to us all and that drifted on the very air

As if drawn by those gently persuasive feelings I got up and began to walk slowly back to the village, strengthened perhaps by that belief in one's own immortality so prevalent in youth. Something told me that nothing very bad would happen to me. And in fact when I came in view of the first straw roofs half-hidden amongst the trees and crossed paths with the first Indians apparently going busily about their work, I felt no surprise at the courtesy and satisfaction with which they greeted me. Some approached and touched me with their usual gentleness, others stopped when they saw me coming and, gesturing enthusiastically, uttered some high-pitched, rapid words of their incomprehensible language including, of course, the eternal *Def-ghi, Def-ghi* which echoed through the sun-dappled shadows.

At last I emerged on to the shore again and was relieved to see that in the pile of hacked up flesh lying on the bed of green leaves there was nothing left to remind me of my companions from the expedition. The heads had gone. As for the grills, they now seemed to be ready for use, as did the pile of firewood that had been gathered in my absence. I moved closer: one of the men was crouching down, and rolling a small pointed stick between the palms of his two hands with practised speed, resting the point on a piece of wood half-covered with dry leaves. After a few minutes this produced a thread of smoke which rose from the leaves until a small but steady bluish flame appeared. The others, who had been watching the Indian crouched over his work, looked pleased and began carefully piling up more dry leaves and twigs around the growing flame and, when the fire had taken, started to add pieces of wood.

As the fire grew, men, women and children came running from the huts and stood staring at the flames. Some gazed with evident delight at the pile of meat. Young and old, men and women, even the children I had seen playing only a short time before by the river, all shared the same simple, untroubled joy at the sight of the fire and the flesh lying on the bed of newly gathered leaves. In that luminous morning they seemed secure, self-contained and enduring, at home in the world, as if it were a space made to their measure, a place where a modest sense of personal finitude accepted its own limits in exchange for a taste of elemental pleasure. I was soon to realize how wrong I was and to discover what black depths lay concealed within those bodies which, in consistency and colour, seemed made of earth and fire.

Three men were using long poles to remove red-hot embers from the heart of the fire and place them under the grills; they tested the temperature by passing the back of their hand slowly over the embers, almost touching them. Finally, when they considered it hot enough, they began to place the pieces of meat on the grill. The torsos and legs had been cut up to make handling and cooking easier; the arms, however, had been left whole. I noticed that there were tiny pieces of some dark substance clinging to the meat and assumed that they must carelessly have dragged the meat along the ground so that dry leaves or twigs had stuck to it. However, when I stepped forward to take a closer look, I realized that, far from being negligent in handling the meat, they had taken special care over it: what I had taken to be extraneous matter picked up from the ground was in fact a dressing made from aromatic herbs intended to enhance the flavour.

The placing of the meat on the grills, which was carried out with ceremonial slowness, attracted even larger numbers of Indians and fired their curiosity still more. It was as if the entire village hung upon those bloodied remains. And the dreamy half-smile on the faces of those who watched in fascination as the cooks worked had the fixity characteristic of any desire whose gratification, for reasons beyond its control, must be deferred and which then engenders within itself a multitude of visions. In the presence of the meat, those Indians burned no less fiercely than the pyre built beside the grills. Although they all wore a similar expression, you could see within each the sudden solitude into which their greedy visions had plunged them, and which, like a victorious army in a conquered city, took possession of even their darkest and most secret places. A child of two or three years approached unsteadily wanting to be picked up. He drummed with his hands on the thigh of some woman, no doubt his mother, and was pushed gently but firmly away. Not for a second did his mother take her eyes off the pieces of meat now sizzling on the fire. The Indians no longer even showed their usual deference towards me, for I seemed to have become invisible to those whose field of vision I crossed. If my body blocked their view of the grill, they simply stepped to one side, giving me a hurried, mechanical smile, merely for form's sake, with the stubborn concentration that typifies desire, which, as I would learn much later, lavishes attention on the loved object simply so as to abandon itself more completely to self-worship, to impossible edifices of its own making, which are related, in that animal ecstasy, to hope.

The only ones who seemed untouched by the general euphoria were the cooks who, with their long poles, fetched embers from the fire to be placed carefully beneath the grill. Calm and attentive, they pored over the finer details of the cooking, peering at the meat as closely as they could despite the smoke stinging their eyes. As fast as the old embers were reduced to ashes, they added fresh ones, extinguishing with short, deft blows the occasional flames that flared up when the dripping fat fell into the fire. Drenched in sweat, they slowly walked round the grills, watching over everything and pausing occasionally to cast a knowledgeable eye over the whole scene. The entire tribe was gathered there and everything, it seemed, had an undeniable reality: the calm, expert cooks, the crowd consumed from within, just as surely as the flames consumed the wood. And, enclosing them, above, below, all around, the sandy earth; the trees stirred not by any breeze but by the short, aimless flights of birds coming and going; the blue and cloudless sky; the choppy waters of the great river; and, over it all, rising slowly, almost at its zenith now, the scorched, blazing sun, of which the fires burning below seemed but fallen, ephemeral fragments. Earth, empty sky, degraded flesh, delirium and the sun above, disdainful yet dependable, for all eternity: that was how, on that morning, reality appeared to my new-born eyes.

I was woken from my reverie by shouts coming from the river: more guests were arriving in large canoes. On hearing them, many who until then had been absorbed in contemplation of the meat ran down to the shore to greet them, adding their own shouts to the hubbub. Some of the new arrivals began chattering before they had even left their boats, not caring whether the people running down the beach towards them could hear or not. Despite the poor stability of the canoes, some were trying to unload enormous jars that took several men to lift. Others jumped from their boats straight on to dry land, carefree and nonchalant, showing no interest in those who came to meet them, so that the two groups, one going from the shore to the grills, the other from the grills to the shore, ran past each other without even exchanging greetings. The first group was drawn ineluctably to the meat, the second to the jars which were being transported with such care and effort. The fifteen or so Indians who had run on up the beach stopped when they reached the cooks and stood staring at the huge grills with the same rather dreamy expression of contained wonderment I had noticed in the Indians already present. Meanwhile those who had gone to meet the canoes dogged the footsteps of those carrying the jars, clustering about them, peering at the contents, leaning slightly forward and huddling together as if struggling to control a shared agitation, though never once offering their help in spite of the evident weight of the jars and the efforts of the carriers not to spill anything. Without pausing for a second by the grills, without even glancing at the seemingly bewitched people lost in contemplation there, the carriers continued walking in the direction of the huts. Once there, they placed the jars in a line in the cool shade of the trees with the same care they had shown in their transportation. Then they turned and walked back to mingle with the people from the village and join them in their contemplation of the grills.

Smoke rose steadily from the meat roasting over the fire. As the fat melted it dripped onto the flames, producing a constant, monotonous sizzling which now and then caused the fire to flare up and smoke even more, so that the vigilant cooks had to lean over to stir the logs with their long poles. Despite the crowd surrounding the grills, the silence of the Indians was so intent that the only sound was the dull crackle of the wood fire and the slowly cooking meat. As well as dense columns of smoke that dispersed only gradually in the air, the meat gave off a powerful but agreeable smell. As the cooking proceeded, the human origins of the meat became less apparent. The skin darkened and split open to reveal, in the vertical cracks that appeared, a reddish, watery juice that oozed out with the fat. Splinters of dry, burnt flesh flaked off the charred parts and the feet and hands, shrunk by the flames, now bore little resemblance to human extremities. An impartial observer would simply have thought they were the remains of some unknown animal.

It is, of course, difficult to speak of these things, but the reader should not be shocked when I say that for a few minutes I felt an overwhelming desire, to which I did not succumb, to know the taste of that unknown animal. Perhaps it was because of the pleasant smell, or because of my accumulated hunger from the night before when the Indians had given me nothing but a little fruit to eat during the journey, or because of those approaching festivities which I, the eternal outsider, did not want to be left out of. Of all the many components that go to make a man, the most fragile is the human element, as enduring and basic as his bones. As I stood motionless amongst the equally motionless Indians, my gaze, like theirs, fixed on the roasting meat, the whole scene lit by the midday sun, it took me a few minutes to recognize that almost against my will, however hard I tried to swallow my saliva, something else, something stronger than repugnance or fear, persisted in making my mouth water.

While the cooking was going on the tribe remained absolutely motionless around the grills, gazing abstractedly, half-smiling, at the meat turning golden-brown amidst the thick columns of heavy smoke that hung in the air. They were so still, these people, so rapt in their adoring contemplation, that I began to walk amongst them, observing them closely as if they were statues. So as not to appear discourteous some made stiff, abrupt gestures in my direction, though without taking their eyes off the meat; only one, bothered by my importunate prowling, muttered something and gave me an impatient look. I walked for a long time amongst those naked bodies and their shrivelled shadows imprinted on the sand by the noonday sun. Eventually, in the midst of the almost total silence, the voice of one of the cooks was heard, no doubt calling the other Indians to approach. A clamour arose from the crowd and they all rushed forward together in a state of febrile excitement, milling about the grills, pushing and jostling for a good place near the cooks.

The imminence of the feast made them anxious: I could see them pressing round the grills, betraying their impatience by the involuntary gestures they made. Some, like children, kept shifting from one foot to the other, as if the very weight of their bodies troubled them; others, if their neighbours so much as brushed against them, reacted by giving them a violent shove. Many scratched their back, head, armpits or genitals with distracted fury; some, balancing on one foot, scratched the dark, muscular calf of the supporting leg with the toenails of the other foot so hard as to draw blood. I was watching from a distance and could only see the outermost circle of the crowd. They were packed so tightly together that the smallest gesture made by one individual set his neighbour rocking, a movement that communicated itself to the rest of the tribe like the spreading ripples of a stone thrown into water. Hence, when the circle nearest the cooks began to move, the whole crowd stirred, following an impulse that seemed common to everyone: to get as close as possible to the grills. This general movement frustrated the efforts of those in the front rows, who, a few moments later, could be seen trying to push their way to the outside, clutching their piece of meat.

The first to appear was a man of indeterminate age with the same shining, lustrous skin as the rest of the tribe; he had the same long, lank hair and muscular legs and arms, his genitals hung forgotten between his legs and his body was entirely hairless but for a sparse scrub of black pubic hair. There was something comical about the way he was holding the piece of meat, which must have been burning his fingers. He was staring at it in rapt concentration; his head was lowered but he managed to raise it for the few seconds he needed to look about him for a suitable place to sit and devour the meat. When he found one – beneath the trees, conveniently close to where the jars had been left in the shade – he sat down on the ground, leaned his back against the trunk of a tree, and started to eat.

Before he took his first bite he seemed to muse upon the hunk of meat, an incredulous expression on his face; it was as if the realization of this longed-for moment satisfied a desire so intense in him that the very immensity of the gift made him doubt its reality. Then, convinced at last by the irrefutable reality of the meat, he began to eat, but every bite taken, far from gratifying his appetite, seemed to increase it. The intervals between bites became shorter and shorter until the rapid nodding of his head made one think less of teeth biting firmly into flesh than of an obstinate, repetitive pecking. He bit into it again and again but, since his mouth was already full of meat he had barely managed to chew, he could only snatch a few greyish filaments which hardly constituted a proper mouthful. It was as if there were in him an excess of appetite which grew as he ate. Worse, the sheer strength of his appetite, expressed in his uncontrollable, repeated gestures, cancelled out or diminished any pleasure he might have gained from his prize. He seemed more of a victim than the piece of meat itself. There was a residual anxiety in him from which the meat was now free. When I looked away from him towards the others, the scene, lit by the harsh sun, instantly reminded me of the feverish activity of an army of ants stripping carrion. A tight knot of bodies was milling around the grills, tense with excitement and impatience. Separated from the central mass of the throng, individuals came and went in search of their first piece of meat, or a second piece if they had finished the first. Meat in hand, they would break away from the dense crowd swarming around the cooks and go off to eat quietly beneath the trees. They resembled ants in other ways too: in the speed with which they walked, in their hesitation before giving way if two of them happened to meet head on,

coming from opposite directions, and even in the rapidity,
frequency and growing anxiety with which they came
and went from the grills.

Their very frenzy to devour the meat seemed to
prevent any of the Indians from enjoying it, as if for
them, guilt, disguised as desire, were the concomitant of
sin. As they ate, the gaiety of the morning began to give
way to a thoughtful silence, to a morose melancholy.
Their chewing kept up the same slow, distracted rhythm
as their plunge into murky, unfathomable thoughts.
Sometimes, one cheek bulging with half-chewed meat,
they would stop eating, lean back against a tree and
remain staring into space for some considerable time.
The feast seemed to be slowly driving them apart. Each
Indian scurried off alone with a piece of meat; they were
just like beasts who, having seized their prey, go off on
their own in order to eat in secret for fear that some
other animal from the pack will snatch it from them. Or
perhaps the origin of the meat they had squabbled over
by the fire aroused in them feelings of shame, resent-
ment and fear. Occasionally, I noticed what seemed to be
a family gathered beneath a tree or in the great open
sandy space that separated the trees from the river.
These groups, set apart from the others, were composed
of old people, adults and children, and in every case one
of the old people or one of the adults was distributing
pieces of meat which they had collected from the grills.
But, although they remained sitting close to each other,
as soon as they received their piece of meat they seemed
to sink into that same sullen silence which affected even
the children. Some faces showed both fascination and
repugnance, repugnance not for the meat but rather for
the act of eating it. However, no sooner had they
finished one piece than they began sucking with relish on

the bones and when there was no more meat to be had they would scuttle off in search of more. They clearly enjoyed the meat, but the act of eating it seemed to fill them with doubt and confusion.

Beneath the sun, which was now passing its zenith and which made the sweating bodies gleam darkly and the slow water of the great river near the shore sparkle, all I could see around me were people chewing. The one exception to the general gluttony was the cooks, who kept a calm and sober watch over the remains of the meat and the fire on which it was cooking. As the guests dispersed, no longer blocking my view of the grills with their jostling bodies, I could see how the cooks with their bone knives were chopping smaller pieces from the large cuts of meat to give to those who approached them, asking for a second or even a third helping. You could tell from the cooks' calm expressions that they, however, had eaten none of the meat.

The meal lasted for hours. In spite of the speed with which they ate, the feast was dragged out by the time spent queuing for another piece of meat or distributing it among the groups gathered under the trees. What also took up time was the stubbornness with which they gnawed every last bit of meat from the bones and, finally, the age they took to swallow down the last few mouthfuls when it was obvious they were already full. Some rested for a while to digest what they had eaten and then went off in search of more.

When the tribe seemed satisfied, a sort of torpor took hold of the bodies scattered beneath the trees. At that point an Indian emerged from behind one of the thatched huts. Judging by the friendly manner in which he approached me, he had evidently not partaken of the meat. He began making rapid but friendly signs for me to follow him. We crossed the wooded area, went past a few huts until, in a plot of land with a few trees in the middle and a series of huts around the edge, we came upon a small group of Indians calmly and quietly grilling some fish. Some of them looked pleased and pointed at me saying, *Def-ghi, def-ghi*, motioning with bunched fingers towards their mouths to indicate that I should eat. The scene was in marked contrast to the one I had been watching on the beach only a few moments before. The easy naturalness with which these men were preparing their meal (over a small grill resting on four logs pushed into the earth), its simplicity, and the generous, paternal way they invited me to share it, all this made me believe for a moment that they could not belong to the same tribe. Slowly, though, I recognized them: they were the men who had been cutting up the bodies. And, as I would realize much later when I had learned the customs of the tribe, they were the men whose arrows had slain the captain and my other companions.

My hosts watched me eat with discreet satisfaction and pleasure – almost, you might say, with tenderness. Delicately and with a generous simplicity they invited me to eat more. In the peace of the afternoon, beneath the cool shade of the trees, these austere figures abandoned themselves to their tranquil memories, swapping friendly monosyllabic remarks from time to time. They were like some hard, round medallion beaten out of a noble metal of which the rest of the tribe, scattered along the beach, were the dark, formless remnants still red-hot from the forge. When our meal was over, my hosts swiftly extinguished the fire, washed, cleaned up the area bounded by the huts and went off, bidding me a courteous goodbye in their shrill, quick voices. Some went off towards the beach, some towards the thick undergrowth behind us, and others into the huts that surrounded the clearing. Sitting alone in the shade, I could hear the voices and noises coming from the beach across the sunny silence. I got up and went towards the river.

Near the grills two men were engaged in a violent argument, their faces so close that they almost touched. They shot furious glances at each other, turned on their heels as if to part for ever, only to wheel abruptly round, their heads so close that at times I feared they would bang them together. Their shrill voices cracked with anger. Finally they stood still and silent, a few inches apart, looking at each other and breathing hard. Their two shadows cast in the same direction by the sun, lay partly overlapping on the yellow ground. Their hostile faces spoke of imminent battle, hatred and scorn. Most startling of all was the apparent indifference of the rest of the tribe – among those who paid them any attention at all, that is, for most were not even looking at the two combatants. The cooks seemed even less interested and in their case the neglect seemed quite deliberate. Their faces turned away, they leaned on their poles looking vaguely in the direction of the river, as if determined to pay no attention to what was happening on the sand; indeed, it was as if they knew all too well and, for some reason unknown to me, were pretending not to. The other members of the tribe, immersed in their stupor, either gazed incuriously at the two men or seemed completely unaware of their presence.

The Indians had finished eating. Now only a few of them – a toothless old man, a child – still sucked thoughtfully on a bone. There was no meat left on the grill. A man holding a bone in one hand mechanically crossed the empty space and tossed it onto the fire. The cooks, leaning motionless on their poles, did not even deign to look at him. The men who had been quarrelling suddenly looked away from each other, walked off in opposite directions and vanished amongst the crowd, which was now seized by a pensive, digestive somnolence. ome were stretched out prone on the ground; others, equally still, stood where they were, their eyes closed, seemingly on the point of collapse. Some had climbed into trees and installed themselves there, trying to fit their bodies to the irregularities of the branches. Their drowsiness seemed to bring them closer to a nightmare than to a dream. Their faces betrayed the persistent visions that were attacking them from within and keeping them from sleep. Their eyes rolled slowly beneath furrowed brows, so that at times they were nearly cross-eyed. They gave sly, furtive glances about them. Though their bodies remained still their toes kept up an involuntary twitching that betrayed what the rest was trying to hide. All their attention was on what was happening inside them, as if they were waiting to see the immediate effect of their feasting and were observing the passage, piece by piece, of every mouthful they had eaten through every inch of their body. It was as if they were convinced that if after a certain time their consumption of the food had no terrible consequences, they could consider themselves out of danger and lay aside their shameful anxiety with impunity. They seemed to hear rising within them a very ancient sound.

About mid-afternoon they began to stir themselves a little. Blinking, they got up, stretched, then ran down to the river where they collapsed again on the ground. They seemed weak and clumsy even when they ran. The children who had been so lively that morning moved with a slowness which could as easily have been the result of ill humour as of sloth. A group of Indians went over to the jars lying beneath the trees and began to examine them with interest from a distance. Some stood on tiptoe and craned their necks to try to catch a glimpse of the contents. Others showed exaggerated signs of impatience. Yet they all seemed serious and withdrawn. Gradually, while still keeping some distance from them, the whole tribe surrounded the jars so that a circle of empty space was left around the trees that shaded them from the sun. The Indians stood staring at them, shifting occasionally from foot to foot to show their impatience. No one spoke to or looked at anyone else. From time to time they would again stand on tiptoe, peering at some point beyond the trees in the direction of the huts. After about half an hour a murmur of satisfaction rose from the crowd: the men who had invited me to eat fish with them were coming down towards us from the huts bringing with them stacks of small bowls. The circle round the jars drew a little tighter. The men with the bowls pushed their way through and piled them up on the ground. In silence they began to fill them from the jars and hand them out to the crowd.

It was clear that it was something alcoholic because, when the Indians drank it, a change - slow in some, immediate in others - came over them. After the first few sips their normal vitality returned and their eyes and faces lit up with something approaching joy. They began to come out of themselves a little, to slough off the sullen, self-absorbed mood into which eating the meat had plunged them. They exchanged a few rapid, friendly monosyllabic words; some even laughed. Their loquacity increased as the vessels emptied. They formed huddles in which they seemed to be telling each other stories or jokes. One of them would talk and, when he had finished, the others, who had been happily giving him their silent attention, would burst out laughing, shaking themselves and giving each other gentle, playful shoves. There was a general and apparently growing mood of gaiety. In the kinder mid-afternoon light, which reflected the glimmering green of the trees back up to the sky, it was strange to see them like that, climbing out from the bottomless pit which they seemed to have fallen into during the meal. The noise of their voices was dissipated in the air and in the yellow light that filtered through the leaves. It was just as with the meat: they kept returning again and again to the jars to refill the bowls, the contents of which they would then down in one go. So great was their euphoria that at times they seemed more likely to unleash some animal howl than to utter any human sound. Their bodies became tense and erect. Their chests swelled, their heads lifted and their arms and legs, which had lost all strength in the lethargy of digestion, regained it with a vengeance, becoming hard and taut, the muscles and veins bulging. Their skin seemed smoother, softer, thicker and healthier. The women's breasts seemed to grow larger, almost to bloom.

This new fullness of their bodies combined with their sudden excitement to draw them into harmony with one another and grew in them like an inner sea, hinting at the imminent drama that would, when it was over, leave them alone again, imprisoned within themselves. What I was most aware of as I watched them was their nakedness. Until only a short time ago this had seemed completely natural to me and yet now, without quite knowing why, I found it troubling. Up to that point their bodies had seemed a self-sufficient, compact whole which concealed itself in unconsciousness and abandon. But as the alcohol took hold, they paraded their naked-ness and were clumsily conscious of it. Their genitals, until then irrelevant, began to stir. The men distractedly handled their own penis or brushed against it, as if by chance, when they dropped one hand to thigh or hip. The women contrived to stand in such a way that their buttocks stuck out or their hips were emphasized. Several of them stroked their own bodies or looked insistently and silently at another's nakedness, as if expecting a reciprocal response. Meanwhile the trips to and from the jars were becoming more and more frenetic; the voices of the Indians grew louder, as if the ancient noise which, hours before, they had been strain-ing to hear in their own bodies, was now building to a shout.

The men who had offered me the fish abstained from the alcohol and confined themselves to serving the others in their usual diligent and efficient manner. They made no attempt to take part in the conversations, nor did they try to impose any order or fairness on the distribution of the brew. An Indian could install himself by the jars and have them fill his bowl five or six times, downing it each time in one go, or he could refill his bowl as many times as he wanted from the jars. The men distributing the alcohol displayed equal indifference in both cases, seemingly imperturbable in the face of the tribe's growing excitement. They appeared distant, absent, as if they and the rest of the tribe belonged to two distinct realities. The others only spoke to them in order to ask for more, although most simply held out their bowl in a peremptory manner.

Like a sun, the Indians' feverish excitement climbed to its zenith. Something was beginning to influence every gesture and every movement, even their laughter. The whole tribe was trembling, seized by an overwhelming emotion. For a while it had seemed merely accidental when one of the men brushed a hand against his penis. But now, as they talked, they distractedly held it in the hollow of their hand and even caressed it. Then a young woman who had been a rather restless participant in one of the small groups suddenly jumped to one side, oblivious of her companions. She stood in a clearing, her feet planted firmly on the ground, her legs apart, her eyes half-closed, and began to move the upper part of her body in slow sinuous movements. She went rigid as a board, caressing her own shining skin with evident delight. At first no one seemed to take any notice of her. The woman cupped her round, dark breasts in her hands and tried, without success, to push them up to within reach of her tongue. She stood on tiptoe as if unaware that this would move her breasts no nearer to her mouth; they simply moved with her, remaining always at the same distance from her tongue. However, that instinctive movement made her whole body seem lither; her muscles arranged themselves differently, her buttocks grew taut and round and a sort of dimple formed where thigh and hip met. Though unable to touch her nipples she continued to flicker her hard, pointed red tongue in and out of her mouth. As it dawned on her that she would never bring tongue and breasts together she began to howl. Observing her breasts, she squeezed them and made circles with them in her cupped hands.

A small, muscular Indian, who had been watching her, came nearer: he had a small, erect, sinewy penis that pressed against his stomach The howling woman was unaware of him, still absorbed in trying to touch her nipples with her tongue. Slowly coming up behind her, the Indian drew nearer, considered her for a moment and then, with a little jump, clasped himself to her, so closely that his erect penis disappeared in the fold between her firm, protuberant buttocks. His arms encircled her and his hands rested on hers as they squeezed her breasts, but the woman continued her distracted howling and her body, shaken by convulsive shudderings, held its position. Nothing in the woman's expression or in her general attitude gave the impression that she had noticed the presence of that small, muscular body that clung to her rounder, more abundant one. The man rested his chin between the woman's shoulder blades and tried with his arms to force her forwards, or even, perhaps, down on all fours, in order no doubt to be able to penetrate her with the small erect penis still lost between her buttocks. But the woman's body remained rigid, legs apart, bottom out, her hands pushing up and squeezing her breasts, her tongue constantly flickering in and out. This, together with her incomprehensible roaring, left on her tongue liquid filaments that escaped from the corners of her mouth leaving parallel trails of mucus or saliva running down either side of her chin. With something akin to fury, the man kept his chin vainly pressed between the two prominent bones of her shoulder blades. The rest of him remained insistently glued to the woman's larger body until she removed her hands from her breasts, stretched her arms away from her body and with an abrupt, unexpected shake freed herself from the man, who fell backwards onto the sandy ground. Scornful, the woman seemed to emerge from her trance and, without a backward glance, calmly walked off towards the trees.

The man lay watching her as if stunned. He seemed neither annoyed nor humiliated by what had happened.

His penis, until a few moments ago so urgently erect and now suddenly detumescent, shrank and disappeared between his legs; his glassy stare was fixed distractedly rather than indifferently on the trees It was clear that the woman who had drawn him to her like magnetic north the compass needle, no longer had any place in his thoughts. Even in mine her presence seemed uncertain. In the transparent light of day, stark and obscene, she had appeared and, having performed her unusual repertoire, had disappeared disdainfully into the crowd. She seemed no less shadowy two or three minutes after her exit than now, sixty years later, as by the light of a candle, the fragile hand of this old man struggles to make real with his quill the images that memory autonomously sends him, who knows how or whence.

Each flicker of the candle flame makes my shadow tremble on the white walls. The window is open to the silent dawn in which the only sound is the scratching of my quill and, now and again, the creaking of my seat or my cramped legs stirring beneath the table. The pages I slowly cover with writing and which I add to those already written, produce a very particular rustling whisper that echoes round the empty room. Always assuming this is not just some post-prandial dream state as fragile as it is transient, it is against this present moment that everything I have lived through laps. Even if the periodically surfacing memories manage to make a crack in that thickness, once what has filtered through has been deposited there like parched dry lava, the heavy persistence of the present closes ranks and the paper becomes once more dumb and smooth, as if untouched by images from other worlds. It is those fleeting, ghostly worlds, no more palpable than the air I breathe, that must have been my life. And yet there are times when the images spring up inside me with such force that the thick wall crumbles and I move between two worlds. The flimsy partition of the body that keeps the two worlds separate becomes simultaneously porous and transparent and it feels as if it is now that I am standing on the great semicircular sweep of beach. Compact, naked bodies cross it, and its soft sand, ruffled by the tracks of blurred footsteps, reveals here and there the parched detritus left by the constant river, the tips of poles blackened by fire or weather, and even the invisible presence of something beyond our experience.

Amongst the Indians there now arose a tumult, which welled up from inside their own bodies and hung in the air amongst the leaves of the trees. That dull tumult filled the entire space, the trees fringing the beach and the sandy floor across which the long blue shadows fell. There was the murmur of tensed limbs, sphincters, pores; to this was added the inaudible breath of unspent sighs that never stirred the outer air, and the hum of resurgent, festering obsessions, of unacknowledged and forbidden desires. Condemned to be suppressed and left to rot in the dank, bottomless blackness of the soul, these oppressive cravings, like a cold, hidden fire, scorched their inner sky and carried them unknowing to their death. The Indians moved seamlessly from languid glances to open caresses. Some lay down on the ground as if to rest, pulling down with them their neighbours who submitted and let themselves fall too. Some opened themselves like flowers or like animals; some walked about among the crowd looking for the object best fitted to their imagination, with the crazed meticulousness of one seeking to match the internal and external worlds, as if the two were made from the same clay. Age, sex or kinship counted for little. A father was as likely to penetrate his own six- or seven-year-old daughter as a grandson was to sodomize his grandfather; a son was as likely to find his own mother seducing him, like some clammy spider, as one sister was to run her tongue, with evident pleasure, over her own sibling's nipples. Here and there, a few solitary figures lying face down on the ground or leaning their backs against a tree abandoned themselves again and again to the pleasures of Onan.

The twilight became filled with panting, muffled cries, with sighs, groans and wailings. Some took their pleasure in twos, others in threes, or in groups of four, five or even a dozen or more. A child of less than seven years old, on all fours, opened her tight vulva with determined fingers and looked provocatively over her shoulder at a big lad who was waiting behind her, holding a fat, smooth, round-ended stick in one hand whilst, in anticipatory pleasure, he stroked his penis with the other. One man was flagellating himself with a switch cut from a tree. Another two, lying on their sides, inverted, languidly sucked each other's penis Others seemed to be coupling with some invisible being. If they were men, they thrust their penis back and forth in the air; if they were women, they would crouch on all fours on the floor, moving their buttocks and writhing as if they really had been penetrated, so much so that you could almost see the moment when the imagined man spilled his seed or else the women would start to moan as if brought to orgasm by a real penis. The woman who shortly before had kept trying to push up her breasts in order to touch her own nipples with her tongue went round repeating her obscene gestures. When anyone approached her she would abandon her vain efforts with the same abrupt scorn and move off, without looking round, in search of a quiet place in which to start all over again.

At nightfall, the Indians who had shared their fish with me lit bonfires. Naked sweating bodies gleamed in the firelight. A fire near the shore was reflected in the river Occasionally, fleeting silhouetted figures in un-equivocal pose would cross the crackling light, only to be lost again in the blackness. A shapeless mass of bodies locked in a multiple embrace rolled, either by accident or design, into a bed of embers and terrible cries mingled with sighs, exclamations and gasps as the squirming bodies sent up a shower of sudden sparks from the fire. Those who had finished made their way, still panting, to find renewed strength and passion in more alcohol from the jars.

Though we mingled with the other members of the tribe, they took so little notice of us it seemed as if any not involved in the orgy had become invisible. They passed us by without so much as a glance or as if we were transparent, their empty gaze looking straight through us in search of something more real on which to rest. It seemed as if we were walking through two different worlds, so that whatever our route, our paths could never cross, as if walls of glass separated us. For example, if a woman came towards us, open and trembling, she would stop short when she reached us, turn and head off in the opposite direction. Or she would walk straight past us, since we, almost instinctively, would step aside at her approach and she would continue along her chosen route as if we occupied no space at all, as if our bodies were not even there to intrude on the emptiness. It was clear that the tribe was embarked on some endless inner journey and that it was only the empty husks of their bodies that drifted from one embrace to the next.

Up above, the stars began to appear like burning coals, one by one at first, then by the handful. They lit up the black sky like so many coloured bonfires – red, yellow, green, blue – their light more tenuous the nearer they were to the huge moon beginning its ascent on the other side of the river. It was a slow-moving moon which, with its broad, fragile swathe of white light, cut in two the empty blackness into which the night had transformed the infinite river, casting harsh, white rays through the trees and illuminating fragments of bodies or groups of bodies or lost faces that fluttered in the dark undergrowth.

On the sand and the countryside surrounding it, amongst thick ashes, charred grass and wood blackened by the fire, the night left a trail of abandoned bodies. Some still writhed, locked in mechanical embraces; some stirred only occasionally; others emitted low moans whilst others again lay completely still. In the tentative dawn an Indian walked across the beach towards the river, repeatedly dabbing at his bleeding nose. One of the Indians was lying motionless, stretched out beneath a tree face down in the sand; I could not decide if he was dead or asleep, even after bending over him for a closer look. As dawn came, first blue then colourless, before the first horizontal bars of sunlight began to tinge the treetops with gold, the Indians started to reappear, vainly attempting to unburden themselves of a weight which seemed to send them reeling back into the very depths of night. Uncertain, they swayed in the sparkling air. Many remained lying down, refusing to move or incapable of getting to their feet: seven or eight of them would never get up again. One man rose, stood still for a few moments, hesitant and thoughtful, then turned round very abruptly and began to beat his head against a tree, harder and harder until he fell to the ground, blood pouring from his mouth and ears. Some lay whimpering on the ground or talked out loud to themselves. When the pale morning settled in, they moved off towards the huts. In the clearing in the middle of these, several vast clay pots were bubbling over a large fire. A handful of men were solemnly stirring the contents; when I went nearer to look I saw that along with some unrecognizable vegetables, they were cooking the viscera and heads of my companions. I went off towards the river again, heading across the crowd that was in the direction of the pots. A man was kneeling on the shore trying to vomit into the water. His eyes were puffy, his face swollen and he was clutching his arms to his stomach as if in pain. I tried to hate him but I could not. When he saw me, his eyes widened a little, betraying who knows what hopes. *Def-ghi, def-ghi,* he murmured, as if wanting to smile or make some gesture, but his body rebelled and, shaken by one final spasm, he fell into the water where he remained for several days, face down in the river, his body rocked by the current.

After consuming the boiled-up viscera and what remained of the alcohol, the Indians' spirits revived somewhat, albeit temporarily. A solitary old woman walked calmly across the beach and sat down on the shore, looking out to the river, gnawing on a head that was almost bare of flesh. All that remained was a skull from which hung gristly strands which she chewed at ineffectually and distractedly with her few remaining teeth. Some strolled about in groups, talking out loud, others, still shaky and restless, crouched down together to form a silent circle, avoiding one another's eyes. One woman, squatting beneath a tree, was pensively defecating. A few scattered groups were still engaged in imperfect and extravagant couplings. Only by mid-morning did they begin to calm down. In the luminous air, a few stragglers were wandering about the yellow beach, seeking some suitable place to rest. Amongst so many prone bodies it was difficult to distinguish who was sleeping, who was dead, or who was simply lost in meditation and breathing quietly, their eyes half-closed. The cooks walked impassively amongst them without once seeming to notice their presence. I stretched out in the shade of a tree and slept until evening. When I woke, the river was almost violet in colour and an Indian was gently trying to wake me. *Def-ghi, def-ghi*, he was saying, brushing my arm with the tips of his fingers. When I opened my eyes he smiled and indicated with a nod that I should follow him. Once again, amongst the huts at the back, the cooks were modestly eating their fish. They cordially invited me to join them and offered me water to drink. The rest of the tribe were still scattered about, deep in torpor.

All through the second night the tumult of the first night was replaced by faltering sighs and sobs, hushed, fleeting conversations, hopeless calls and laments. They spoke little and then only slowly. When I walked amongst them they followed me with their eyes, as if they lacked strength for anything more. After a while they would simply shake their heads and lower their eyes; some even began to sob. They were like sick, abandoned children. At daybreak I stumbled on one lying on his side on the ground. He was making drawings in the sand with a twig, only to erase them immediately with a sweep of his hand. He spent all day doing this.

Many seemed ill. Some grimaced in pain, tentatively touching their own bodies; others lay on the ground tormented by diarrhoea or gasping for breath like asthmatics or dying men. Their half-closed eyes were puffy, their faces swollen, their hair dull and greasy. Many were wounded or had burns on their skin. The arm of one man hung loosely at his side as if broken at the elbow. Many were limping or even dragging themselves from place to place. I saw them going repeatedly down to the river where they would crouch to wash their faces or splash their bodies with water. Those who were wounded or ill gave vent to their pain by breathing out hard between clenched teeth so that their saliva bubbled. One man, leaning against a tree, kept spitting again and again; another defecated and then applied himself to scrutinizing his excrement, turning it over with one finger. The high spirits of the previous days had been spent, leaving them fearful and battered. It was as if, having loosed its arrows, the bow of desire had recoiled in their bruised, stunned faces. The young seemed old and the old young; the women had become as rough and graceless as men and the men soft and fragile as women. On many faces red spots with white pus-filled heads had sprung up. Wherever I looked I could see only furtive eyes and weary flesh. They were like dark, dubious stains on the steady brilliance of summer: by contrast, the night, with its immense moon and numberless stars, seemed healthy and full of light. But the cooks, with their calm good sense and clean, hard bodies, had remained clear and compact throughout, and were proof that the Indians had the necessary strength to protect themselves from the indeterminate.

In the days that followed they emerged slowly but painfully from their self-absorption. Many took weeks or even months to do so, and there were many deaths in the tribe during this time. Serious and sobered they began to rouse themselves and to clean up the fields and the beach; they set about taking care of the sick, whom they carried inside the huts, and burying the dead. They went to and fro amongst the trees, absorbed in what they were doing, exchanging only essential phrases in their shrill voices. They never showed any feeling, remaining grave, almost severe. They bathed in the river, made tools from wood and bone, and performed all those actions which gave them and the place in which they lived that irrefutable, dense physical presence, so palpable to the senses and so apparently immutable. It was this presence I had sensed from the canoe when I first approached the half moon of beach and the traces of human sounds and smells drifting across to me from the fires scattered in the growing dark. Two or three days had sufficed to show me the black depths from which those Indians had to drag themselves, up towards the transparent air, in order to present a human face to the outer world.

The whole tribe was like a sick patient making a slow recovery from illness. Those who took a long time to recuperate or who died were like the horribly damaged or irrecoverable parts of a single being. Their bodies were like the visible symptoms of an invisible malaise. The wounds, physical debility and deathly pallor, the blood, pustules and burn marks were merely the outward signs of some arbitrary power ruling them from the blackness. It was something present in and evenly distributed amongst them all, one substance in respect of which each of the Indians, seen as individuals, seemed fragile and incidental. I don't know which god it was, if it was a god, for in all the years I was there I never saw the Indians worship anything. It was a presence which governed them in spite of themselves, which had more power over their actions than their will or their good intentions and which, every now and then, would reveal itself, however hard the Indians tried to forget or ignore its existence, like the leviathan which can be seen periodically as it rises from the ocean depths.

A week later, most of the sick had recovered and it was already difficult to distinguish the calm, healthy cooks from the rest of the tribe. A few still left their huts only slowly and hesitantly; each morning they could be seen standing at the entrance, screwing up their eyes in the bright sun, looking rather dazedly at the glittering leaves, leaning against the wall of the hut or supported by a friend. Many were scarred for ever: one had lost an ear, another an eye which continued to suppurate for many months, a third would be lame for the rest of his life. Sometimes, passing them on the beach or in the woods, and seeing that they were maimed and carried in their own body the unequivocal evidence of their excesses, I would look at them questioningly to see if some gesture, expression or grimace might indicate that the embers of those dreadful days still burned in their memories. But their eyes seemed dumb and innocent as they met mine, indifferent or inaccessible to memory. There was no sign of complicity or connivance either, in the quick, almost ironic smile they would give me, as if in accepting my testimony they also recognized the delicacy of my silence or as if, on meeting my insistent, questioning gaze, their very impenetrability gave them some sense of superiority. On the contrary, the smile seemed to have nothing to do with the acts they had committed and which I had witnessed; rather it seemed to refer to certain actions which they believed me capable of and which they hoped I might some day undertake. Once the storm was over, the tribe again treated me with cordiality and deference. There are those who believe that our first impressions are the truest and most accurate: but I must say that in this case such a statement does not hold true. As time passed the Indians, who in those first days had behaved worse than wild beasts, became the most chaste, sober, balanced beings I have ever encountered.

The delicacy of this tribe could almost be thought effeminacy or prudishness, their cleanliness a mania, their consideration for their fellow man ostentatious affectation. This exaggerated urbanity grew as the days passed, reaching ridiculous heights of complexity. They were extraordinarily modest. In the months that followed I never saw a single Indian relieve him or herself in public. Despite the fact that the men were completely naked, I never saw any male, child or adult, whose penis betrayed any other state or function than that of hanging limp, almost non-existent and half-hidden between their legs. Fondling, touching and any kind of sexual innuendo seemed to be excluded from their relations in public. Their circumspection in this regard was so great that even now I ask myself if they ever fornicated, even in private; and had it not been for the births which occurred throughout the year even the most perspicacious observer would have concluded that those Indians knew nothing of sexual intercourse. In addressing each other, men and women were distant and evasive, even when they belonged to the same family. Their treatment of their children was solemn, severe and curt, although neither harsh nor authoritarian, and certainly not without consideration or even affection. In general there was a separation, with the women and children on one side and the men on the other. All of them were excessively, almost irritatingly careful about cleanliness. A child of one or two years old, walking around with its bottom smeared with excrement, was certain to cause an argument between husband and wife; a child caught urinating against a tree in full public view would be sure to get its ears boxed.

As I have just mentioned, apart from during the orgies I never saw them urinate or defecate in public, nor did I ever come across their excrement anywhere near the huts and after a while I realized why: they buried it. They did not just cover it up summarily with a little earth but dug a small hole in the ground and piled enough earth over it to hide any trace. When it was hot they used to bathe in the river several times a day, so that the yellow beach was always full of people and when I walked along the shore I would see them continually entering and leaving the water and if by chance I found myself in earshot but out of sight of the river I could still hear the noise of them splashing all day and even at night. In winter they heated up water in their clay pots and washed with that, but quite a few still bathed in the river, walking casually down to the shore, unperturbed by the blue dawn frost. They untiringly washed and rewashed all their food before cooking it. They swept their huts and the surroundings several times a day with brooms made from branches and on summer evenings they damped down the ground inside and out, bringing water from the river in their jars, sprinkling it with their hands, making it sparkle in the late evening light.

They were obliging to the point of ostentation and tedium. Though, as generally happened, they were hard at their daily tasks, anyone who passed near their hut was greeted insistently and invited to stop for a moment at the entrance. They would then begin a long inter-rogation the aim of which was to elicit full information about the state of health of each and every relative of the passer-by. They would demand detailed replies and encourage more extensive responses with supplementary questions, thereby ensuring that the whole ceremony lasted an hour or more, with the owner of the house even demanding news about the health of people he had seen that same morning on the beach and with whom he had exchanged greetings from afar. When these chance encounters occurred in the public area, that is to say, somewhere away from the huts of those involved, they would limit themselves to a brief, laconic, almost haughty dialogue. Maintaining a distance was also, it seems, important, for they would stand about two or three yards apart, as if their main concern was not to touch each other, to avoid physical contact at all costs They would remain erect and dignified for a few seconds, their shoulders slightly back, exchanging brief formulae totally lacking in warmth and sincerity and then continue on their way, their heads held high, their eyes half-closed, back and shoulders rigid in a conventional attitude of seriousness and pride. This excess of dignity made them susceptible and the least significant things caused them offence. If, for example, a mildly shocking allusion was carelessly introduced into a conversation, those present would lower their heads, adopt a pensive air, remain silent for a while and then, after a moment, find a pretext to withdraw. Before touching on any topic connected with fornication, menstruation or excrement they made sure the children were out of the way; anyone who flippantly started talking about one of these subjects without ensuring that the smaller children were out of earshot was called to order in no uncertain terms.

Gradually the Indians returned to their rapid way of doing everything, as if they had required a certain period of time to relearn it. This rapidity of movement was typical only of the men, for the women moved about calmly and dreamily and performed all their tasks as if their minds were on something else. The men did everything virtually at a run, and when they passed any women the difference in speed was startling. It was as though the men were the tough, rotating horizon of a dark, soft and sedentary centre represented by the women When men stopped to exchange their laconic formalities on the yellow beach, the speed of their movements was such that they always seemed to be making little leaps on the spot, at a safe distance from each other, as if they were forbidden ever to stand completely still. For example, when they went fishing, they would run across the beach, leap into their canoes and paddle energetically away; a few minutes and they would have disappeared along one of the smaller rivers formed by the islands. They kept up a constant, regular pace so that they appeared to do everything in a rush, and when night came they lay down on the newly swept floor of their huts and slept until dawn.

In the sunny mornings they filled the translucent air with their comings and goings. The only reminder of those first days were the few maimed Indians I glimpsed amongst the others. They were a polite, hardworking, austere tribe. They joked little and, apart from the children, who generally played outside the settlement, hardly ever laughed. The women seemed less serious or perhaps slightly less rigid than the men. The men's attitude bordered on sullenness, while that of the women seemed more like resignation or indifference. Men and women alike seemed to do things out of a sense of duty, not because they wanted to. Pleasure seemed entirely absent from community life. It was certainly not because of any lasciviousness in their public lives that one knew that in private they did at least copulate. The only proof of that were the women's swelling bellies and the wrinkled bloodied children who emerged now and then into the sun of their world.

Treated attentively and indifferently by turns, or with sudden, fleeting obsequiousness, the object of incomprehensible demands or of persistent disdain, I drifted amongst them, convinced that what they seemed to expect of me (if, that is, they expected anything at all) would not be achieved through my death but rather through my constant presence and my patient attention to their harangues. Occasionally an Indian would approach me, plant himself in front of me and embark on an interminable discourse full of slow, explanatory gestures indicating the horizon, the river, the trees, every so often bending his arm and energetically striking his chest with the palm of his hand to signify that he was the centre of this stream of short, shrill, rapidly spoken words. On other occasions, I would be brought up short as I was passing a hut by the voice of a woman working in the shade by the door, murmuring *Def-ghi, def-ghi* in a soft, confiding tone. Without looking up from her work, the woman would deliver a short, precise speech and then, without once having looked at me, go on working in silence as if I were already gone. The children were more expansive and would sometimes follow and talk to me. They were like the rowdy reverse side of the tribe, but even they were affected by the general air of seriousness, which dampened their enthusiasm.

The weeks and months passed. Autumn came. A storm swept away the summer and after the rains the light seemed paler, more dilute. During the sunlit afternoons, amongst the ceaselessly falling yellow leaves that lay rotting at the foot of the trees, I would sit quite still on the ground, meditating on the uncertain fascination of the visible. Then the tenuous, uniform light would seem even purer against the yellow foliage and the clear blue sky and almost white amongst the faded grass and the dry, silky, bleached sand; the sun, warming my head, seemed to melt the confining mould of habit and neither affection nor memory, nor even the strangeness of everything, gave any sense or order to my life At such times the whole world, to which in this ulterior stage of my life I give the name of autumn, would rise clearly before my senses from its dark other side and show itself to be part of me, part of everything I was, so irrefutable and natural that we were held together only by a sense of mutual belonging untrammelled by any potential obstacles such as excitement, fear, reason or madness. And later, when the sun began to decline and mundane thoughts caught me up in their redeeming arbitrariness, I would stroll amongst the Indians looking for some useless task that would get me through to the end of the day. Then I would once again become the abandoned one, with a name and a memory, a network of pulses beating at the heart of things.

Winter brought with it an element of reality. The alternating frosts and drizzle reminded us of our human vulnerability and drove us to build some means of protecting ourselves against the world. Maintaining the huts, tanning the hides and feeding the elemental fire around which we crowded, were all part of our struggle to recover some animal warmth and to survive. And it kept us occupied in practical tasks that took our minds off things impossible to speak of. The Indians suffer hardship with dignity: the little sustenance they can wrest from winter is shared out equally, and the strongest among them form a protective wall around the weakest, giving them food and life. They show discernment and discretion in everything they do; much later, I realized that the reason some of the stronger men enjoyed certain privileges during the months of scarcity was not because others feared their brute strength, but because those men were necessary for the survival of the whole tribe, every one of whose members, down to the humblest, from the newborn to the dying, had been given a particular role to play. In surprising contrast to the horror of my first days there, I often saw one of those strapping men give up his cloth or his share of the food to someone old or sick, or to a child.

Thus did the Indians behave in the harsh, grey winter, though never losing their habitual sullenness and shyness. Every day a man brought something to eat and some firewood to the hut that was set aside for me and which stood slightly apart from the others. He never spoke. I should also say that of all the winters I spent amongst the Indians, the first was the longest and the hardest. For weeks the icy drizzle obliterated both horizon and sky and when at last it ended, the cold increased instead of diminishing. Night after night, from a sky so clear and so close it seemed to be pressing down on us, the frosts fell, so that each morning the day dawned on white fields, as if the stars, pulverized by the cold, were gradually disintegrating and sprinkling the earth with stardust. Apart from the great river, every expanse of water was covered by a thin, fragile layer of glittering ice, blue at dawn, yellowish green during the day and pink in the evening. Even the sand became finer, as if it too were made of stellar dust; and the earth, parched and hard where it was not mixed with sand, became shiny and tinged with blue. For weeks a kind of quiescence reigned, as if the air and even time itself were frozen, as if the very light had stopped still or become pure transparency, like the ice through which its changes were filtered and reflected, blue, green, yellow, violet, rose and red. The trees seemed petrified and the bare crisscrossing branches, black against the whitish sky, formed a nightmare landscape. Animals and birds froze and lay grey, stiff and preserved, caught between the cold and death. In those endless nights many people met the same fate, especially the old: overwhelmed by cold and sleep and with no desire to leave their beds, they would journey on to death out of pure laziness or expediency. In the cruel winter they fell towards death lightly, silently, painlessly, as the leaves in autumn fall towards their true home, the earth. The survivors watched for a warm breeze to come from the uncertain north. And when the first tender, red-tinged leaves began to appear, it seemed as if it was the frozen air itself and not the buds that burst asunder.

Little by little, the Indians began to leave their huts, to venture forth not just into the open air but into the spring itself. The air thawed just as the ice became water and the crystalline trees began to put out slow clouds of green leaves into the blue air. The flower-filled fields were soon busy once more with the rapid comings and goings of the Indians. The sand grew yellow again and the river turned to gold. Flocks of multicoloured birds flew stiffly out from the islands, streaking the blue sky and crowding the trees in the fields behind the village. Pumas and alligators made their sleepy reappearance. The warm days stretched into long evenings of ruddy skies. Each day, as the spring advanced, people lingered later along the shore, so that in that season of hope the smells of cooking, the slow walks along the river shore, the yellow gleam of the first stars in a still, clear sky and

the light that formed a nimbus about the foliage of the
trees made the evenings calm and benevolent. By mid-
morning, when the cold had lost its edge, the first fires
were lit, first outside, in front of the huts, then amongst
the trees, and then all over the settlement. It was still full
of the debris of other seasons that lay rotting or buried,
worn thin by time and rain – leaves, wood, the bodies of
animals, human flesh and bones, excrement. Slow,
victorious plumes of smoke began to rise again amongst
the budding branches, bringing with them, as well as all
the other feelings they aroused in those from whom the
privations of winter had driven out all sense of self, the
memory of an ancient will to endure. After months of
withdrawal and somnolence, it was good to see us going
out into the world again on mornings ever warmer and
sunnier. The luminous days seemed to infect those stiff,
circumspect beings with euphoria and even happiness.
They seemed to go about their work motivated by
something more joyous and congenial than duty,
efficiency and survival; and when they passed each other
on the shore or amongst the trees, they stayed to talk a
little longer than usual as if they no longer considered
courtesy offensive or merely feckless, and the austere
pleasure they shared was proof of their superiority over
time and things.

As time passed, however, the sweetness began to cloy.
The onset of summer was like stepping into a house of
fire; we revolved dazed and lost in the white light. The
sticky shade of the trees no longer provided shelter.
Only in the early hours was it a little cooler, for the first
light of dawn brought with it a burning heat that lasted
until well into the night. The tribe tossed and turned in
an unquiet sleep. In the preceding months the Indians
had gone to bed early in order to rise at dawn fresh and

ready for work. At night not a soul stirred about the settlement: a peaceful silence reigned, interrupted only by the cries of night birds. With the coming of the intense heat the spontaneous discipline broke down. At first I attributed it to the arid sun that rose again and again in a limitless sky. But gradually I came to realize that just as evening heightens the dying man's fever, the passing year was dragging with it from some unknown place of darkness a throng of half-forgotten, half-buried things, the persistence and even existence of which seemed impossible to us. Yet, when they resurfaced, they forced us to see by their urgent presence that they had always been the only reality of our lives. Just as, after months of quiet, the gradual violence of its floods, the detritus and strange beasts swept along on its waters, reveal the pent-up violence of the great river.

The normally cool, courteous relations between the Indians began to break down in whispered confidences, indifference and brawling. Many grew impatient and irritable, and most became withdrawn, wandering about like lost souls or sleepwalkers They evidently found the wine of those dawns too potent. It seemed to ferment grief and nostalgia in them. It was obvious that they were lacking something, but as I was only able to see them from the outside, I could not fathom what. They kept a watchful eye on the blank day, the clear sky, the luminous coast, in the hope of receiving some message or revelation from the dancing air. With nothing to cling to, they drifted in passive expectancy. The common substance that glued the tribe together, that gave them the cohesion of a single being, grew weaker, threatening them with aimlessness and dispersion. They were vacant and morose in their day-to-day treatment of one another. They sensed a lack they could not name; they were seeking without knowing what they sought or what they had lost.

But when they did understand, every gesture became a message or a sign; slowly, with increasing confidence, they prepared for action. I could read in their faces and attitudes their growing sense of determination. Passing a hut one day I saw an old woman contemplating a skull, dry and polished with age. Undisguised ardour and fascination were written on the old woman's wrinkled face. In the days that followed I often saw groups of Indians plotting together, while others moved singly from group to group, conveying messages and ideas. Others prepared poison arrows with skilful eagerness. The belongings of the captain and my companions began to reappear in different places, who knows from where: clothing, a helmet, a sword, pieces of armour, coins. Everyone wanted to look at them, to touch and handle them. In less than a year they had acquired the shabby, definitive look of relics. For the privilege of a brief contact with them fights would break out and blood was spilled. They were mixed up with objects I did not recognize but whose origin was easy to guess at: necklaces, gemstones, knives and pieces of wood so polished and yellowed that it was difficult to distinguish them from the jumble of bones, both animal and human to judge by the different shapes and sizes, they were stored with. Sometimes during one of the frequent, violent skirmishes a skull would roll across the sand. Yet no one held the objects in their hands for long. As well as the immense attraction those objects held for the Indians, it seemed as if they also exuded some deadly poison.

One morning, very early, a noise woke me. It was barely dawn. In the blue air of the beach, gleamed a crowd of dark bodies agitated by anxiety, impatience, enthusiasm, perhaps even joy. About a hundred men were embarking in the canoes lined up on the shore and the whole tribe was present to see them off. Everyone was chattering in low voices and gesticulating, somewhat constrained by repressed excitement. The canoes left the shore almost simultaneously – almost the instant the men leaped on board – and they moved off upriver, all at the same speed, until lost amongst the islands. The rest of the tribe remained on the beach for a long time afterwards, as if in amazed and hopeful contemplation of the huge red sun which was rising beyond the islands, banishing the darkness from the morning air and sowing the violet-coloured river with fragile lights.

As the days passed people's eyes turned repeatedly towards the great river, shining and empty. The low islands it had formed lay unmoving in its centre, stretching upriver. Not a breath of cool air came from the water. And on the horizon, white and hazy in the heat, there was not so much as a suggestion of a sign. Growing uncertainty and anxiety gnawed at the Indians' hearts. Now and then one of them would leave what he was doing and go down to the beach on the pretext of washing his hands or urinating into the water. From there he would look furtively upriver in the hope of seeing the return of the canoes. Others went out several times a day to survey the water from the door of their hut where the shade protected them from the heat. Gradually their impatience drove them to abandon their tasks so they could keep a watch on the shore. At first there were only three or four of them, the second day a handful, the third almost a crowd; by the fourth, the whole tribe was on the beach, their eyes fixed on the flat, elongated islands between which the canoes had disappeared and through which they doubtless hoped to see them reappear

And they did return, though not at dawn as when they had set off. Their shining blue figures appeared at nightfall, as they had when they first brought me back with them. This time I watched the lighting of the bonfires whose flames I had seen illuminating the beach on that first occasion. Everything was exactly the same only now these events mingled with other similar events unfolding in my memory. There was a familiar flavour about what was coming. It was as if, starting again, time had moved me along to another point in space from which I could view the same cyclical repetition of events from a different perspective. I watched the boats cleaving the blue air and heard the fast, steady rhythm of their paddles in the water which was full of reflections from the fires. The impression of it all having happened before was so strong that for a few minutes I was filled, almost without realizing it, with the intense, wholehearted expectation that I would see myself, lost and as if bewitched, slowly rediscovering the infinite darkness I had only glimpsed the first time I saw those shores in that blue night so full of apparent peace and human bustle.

It was not me arriving in those boats but someone else, a man possibly about my age, standing stock still amongst the rowers. As soon as he touched land, some of the Indians were already calling out to him: *Def-ghi, def-ghi*. The general confusion and the crowd prevented the villagers from getting near the bodies that the expedition was unloading from the boats and piling unceremoniously onto the sand. The prisoner – the word, as will become evident, is inappropriate – ignored them and, if he deigned from time to time to look on anyone, he did so with calculated disdain and scornful indifference. The

others kept on calling out: *Def-ghi, def-ghi,* pointing to
themselves in the hope of catching his eye. They gave
him the same cloying smiles that I knew so well, played
the same feeble tricks, pretending to be angry and
aggressive, for example, only to collapse in loud laughter
minutes later; they mounted the same theatrical display
intended to portray themselves as ostentatiously visible
people. The prisoner deliberately ignored these attempts
at seduction, but this only encouraged the Indians,
provoking them into such a variety of reactions that at
one point it was hard to tell whether the change of
attitude was genuine or feigned, or whether they rang
the changes on purpose, passing from hilarity to rage,
from sentimentalism to violence, from haughtiness to
obscenity, in search of some instantly recognizable pose
they could adopt. It may also have been that they were
genuinely provoked by the prisoner's indifference and by
the anxiety, uncertainty and confusion that his presence
seemed to arouse in them. Because of this they were like
some soft, formless material moulded by constantly
shifting circumstance into arbitrary, ephemeral shapes.
One thing, however, was certain: the prisoner knew
from the very first what the Indians expected of him,
something which I grasped only very gradually and after
a long time. Even now, sixty years later, writing by
candlelight on this summer night, I am not entirely sure I
have understood, even though I have spent my whole life
pondering the real nature of their hopes.

What happened in the days that followed can all too
easily be guessed: from the burgeoning desire in the
quiet, sunny morning while the dismembered bodies
were grilling over the fires to the scattering of dead and
wounded three or four days later, and the tribe's hesitant
new beginning, passing through the contradictory

pleasures of the feast, the suicidal resolve of the drinking spree and the quagmire of their multiple couplings, frenetic and bizarre. The identical repetition of this sequence of events was still more surprising when one realizes that it seems to have been entirely unpremeditated, that the events were undetermined by any previous plan and that the grey, measured, joyless days of the Indians had been carrying them, all unknowing, towards that fiery resolution which was their one celebration, from which many emerged battered and barely alive and in which some remained entangled for ever. It was as if they danced to and were ruled by a silent music, the existence of which the Indians sensed but which was inaccessible and dubious, at once absent and present, real if indeterminate, like that of a god.

Like my shadow, the prisoner, somewhat forgotten, walked about the large sandy clearing where the fires were still smoking. I had spent my first day wandering amongst the tribe in fear and amazement; this prisoner, however, seemed not only calm and indifferent but even, if the attitudes he adopted were to be believed, a little disappointed that the Indians, absorbed in their contemplation of the meat or lost in carnal dreams, took so little notice of him. He appeared to expect flattery and submissiveness from them and was visibly vexed when they failed to make enough fuss of him. It was as if the fact of his capture gave him a certain sense of superiority It is true that the moment he disembarked many of the Indians had gone up to him and gathered round him and generally done everything they could to attract his attention; I could see that he would be besieged, as I had been during my first days and weeks in the village. However, unlike me he seemed to understand perfectly the reasons for this and showed by his haughty,

disdainful manner that the siege did not bother him in
the least; instead, for reasons I could not fathom, it
conferred on him some unknown power. What was
clear, however, was that my presence irritated him. The
contemptuous looks he gave me, so different from the
studied, imperious gaze he bestowed on the rest of the
tribe, were thick with hatred. I often caught him
watching me furtively, like someone studying the
enemy. He tended to avoid my gaze as if by not looking at
me directly and ignoring me he could magically establish
my non-existence in this world where my very presence
seemed to thwart him. When I saw him arrive, another
survivor in exactly the same situation as myself, I
thought the far horizon had at last sent me an ally, but,
from the moment he spotted me amongst the tribe, he
was never less than evasive or hostile. He understood.
He knew the score not only as regards his own role,
which he performed with a kind of prolix fervour, but
also as regards mine; I had the rather disagreeable sense
of being both included and rejected by him. When, in
brief moments of lucidity, the Indians returned to the
siege, the prisoner would act like some very important
man reluctantly condescending to pay heed to the
petitions of the people and then equally capriciously
returning to his loftier concerns without once revealing
whether he intends to take the petitions into account in
any future decisions or even whether he has, in fact,
heard them. His attitude exasperated the Indians who at
times gave up pleading and resorted to making urgent
demands and even threats. But it was clear their anger
did not frighten the prisoner. He seemed to dominate the
whole tribe merely by virtue of a repertoire of affected
poses. The cooks (different men from the last time)
treated him with the same calm courtesy they had shown

towards me, but even with them he was impossible. Still today I find myself wondering if his outrageous behaviour was a character trait or an act he put on – today, tonight, all these years later, when I think I know what the Indians expected of me, having slowly worked it out over the years. The prisoner understood right from the start either because he belonged to a neighbouring tribe and knew the language of his captors, or because his own tribe had been the object of similar raids; having heard about it from others, he must have been fully aware of the reasons for his captivity. This bestowed on him a privilege which, it must be said, he frequently abused. As far as I could see, he was not above extortion and unblushingly accepted all kinds of gifts without, however, promising those who gave the gifts that their wishes would be granted. He enjoyed this comfortable position for a couple of months until one drizzly autumn morning he left in a canoe loaded down with food and trinkets, and disappeared, paddling slowly upriver, silent and erect, never for an instant having lost the ill-humoured, scornful air of one who disdains to be the guest of inferior people undeserving of his illustrious presence. He remained impassive in the face of the clamouring tribe, who escorted him to the canoe like a sovereign prince, each face and gesture betraying their heartfelt need to win his respect and a place in his memory. In the late autumn, in the monotonous grey of earth, air, water and sky, he slowly vanished beyond the horizon, becoming part of it, one more mirage in a world which furnishes us with so many.

By that time the Indians had made the slow, painful climb out of the black hole into which they periodically plunged. I lived with them for ten years and ten times I saw them seized by the same madness. What I found most extraordinary was that during the months of abstinence they gave no outward sign of the immense force of the desire devouring them. Though it took me a long time, I did eventually begin to find my way through the jungle of their language and to make rather rough and ready use of it. To satisfy my curiosity I would ply them with oblique questions but it was as if they had lost all memory and had no idea what I meant. There was nothing evasive or hypocritical about their replies: they had either simply forgotten or knew nothing about it. The Indians never lied. They spoke little and always with good reason. The art of conversation was unknown to them. The discussions they held were not really conversations, more an exchange of very precise ideas which they would throw out to the others and which would be received in silence. Sometimes hours would pass between a question and its answer and the verbal frenzy that occasionally overtook these meetings was due not to the large number of speeches made but to the repetition, at different pitches and speeds, of two or three short, shrill phrases, or even of a single word. The conventional greetings they exchanged with one another and the proliferation of polite formulae they considered a necessary evil. Their verbal parsimony seems sufficient proof to me that they did not lie, because in general lies are forged in language and require an abundance of words in order to flourish. Their forgetfulness and their ignorance seemed genuine: it was as if part of the dark land they traversed had entered and coloured their minds, masking with blackness memories which, had they remained too near the surface, would have driven them mad. Their exaggerated prudishness doubtless came from an unconscious, confused animal fear of one day glimpsing the horrors they might be capable of.

During the months when hardship forced them to confront the outside world they forgot everything and reverted to their old austere, fraternal selves, motivated less perhaps by any noble thoughts than by an unacknowledged realization that the strength and unity of the tribe were vital to the celebration of their carnal rites. The rot set in with the end of winter. Interminable days of blinding light would confront their abandoned and naked selves with the unforgiving evidence. Just as they passed from apathy to frenzy, so they passed not simply from one season to the next but from one world into another, one where they would once again forget everything: family ties, modesty, restraint. To do so they journeyed through a dark region, like the waters of oblivion, until at last they reached a point, beyond all barriers, on the brink of annihilation. It was inevitable that some would not return and that many of them would emerge badly burned, like people who had walked through fire. This constant ebb and flow was, I think, a source of great unhappiness to them. You only had to see how the long-desired object burned their fingers even as they held it. And their circumspection during the months of abstinence came from a sense that everyday actions were mere appearance and that they, the Indians, belonged to a forgotten world. From the day they were born until the day they died, the Indians wandered that vast land like lost souls. The ubiquitous fire that consumed them burned both in each individual and in the tribe as a whole. It was a single fire whose flames did not burst suddenly into life at different times in each of them but instead burned constantly in all at all times, only now and then showing itself. Tossed on the incandescent breath of that fire they were no more masters of their actions than the dust whirled up by a

November storm. I grew up amongst them and my initial feelings of horror and repugnance were slowly replaced by compassion. They were battered by one force, made up of hunger, rain, cold, drought, floods, disease and death, that existed within another larger power that ruled over them with its own peculiar and excessive rigour against which they had no defence. Since the latter force was hidden they could not, as they could against the former, make weapons or build shelters that might attenuate its impact. I knew they were capable of great resistance, generosity and courage and were skilled in the manipulation of the known world: one had only to see the implements they used and the skill with which they were fashioned and employed to understand at once that the Indians were not intimidated by the harshness of nature. However, they were like a raft of shipwrecked sailors struggling to maintain discipline on board as a storm rages in the dead of night.

There are many days, hours and minutes in ten years. Many deaths and births too. As I was changed and shaped by the flow of time, what had seemed strange to me when I stepped on to the beach that first night slowly became familiar. It is hard for any of us to locate our past with any certainty in a precise moment in time and space. Coming as I do from nothingness, I find the reality of my past even more problematic. No human life is longer than those last seconds of lucidity that precede death. Twenty, thirty, sixty, or even ten thousand years of past life are of the same duration, the same reality. However huge the fire the only truth it leaves is ashes. But there is in every life one decisive moment, which is, no doubt, also pure illusion, but which nonetheless gives us our definitive shape. It is an illusion slightly more substantial than the others, which is given to us so that when we proffer it as an explanation, we have some sense of what the word 'life' means. I was soft clay when I reached those dreamlike shores and adamantine rock when I left, despite the fact that given my age now, my time there was relatively short and even though in the years that followed I have apparently lived a life which others might think significant and interesting.

Because I lived amongst the Indians for a long time, my life there was quite unlike the splendid sojourn enjoyed by other prisoners kept for a few months before being sent off in canoes loaded down with presents towards the far horizon of the river. Whilst it is true I was the recipient of their unostentatious protection and of some privileges, I shared with them good times and bad, though they had the sense to leave me out of their gross festivities. On the last few occasions I avoided these by going off alone into the countryside for three or four days, not because I found the festivities so repugnant but because it grieved me to see people who had often shown me consideration and kindness and for whom I felt some affection falling again into the same blackness. Learning their language was all the more difficult because of its rudimentary nature. It might have seemed to a casual observer that the language was invented according to the caprice of each individual speaker. Later I realized that we impose laws even on caprice just to give ourselves the illusion of knowledge. In that aspect too the lives of the Indians were markedly different from those of other men amongst whom I had lived and would live. Their life and the language they spoke tasted to me of the planet itself, of the human herd, of a world not infinite but unfinished, of undifferentiated, confused life, of blind, structureless matter, of a silent firmament: a taste, as they say, of ashes. For years I woke up day after day not knowing if I was a beast or a worm or just a lump of dormant metal, and I would spend the whole day in this state of doubt and confusion, as if entangled in an obscure dream full of cruel shadows from which only the oblivion of night freed me. But now that I am old I realize that the blind certainty of being a man and nothing but makes us more like beasts than does that feeling of constant, almost unbearable doubt over our own condition.

Very slowly I came to see that world of water, sand, vegetation and sky as a definitive place.During the first months, perhaps even the first two or three years, my eyes were continually scanning the horizon for something that would rescue me not so much from the poverty of my existence there as from its strangeness. But that hope faded with the years. The deceptive solidity of daily life gnawed away at my rigid, defenceless memories. There can be no doubt that when we forget, it is not so much a memory we lose as our desire to remember it. Nothing is innate in us. However neutral and grey the new life we accumulate, it is still enough to cause our most steadfast hopes, our most intense desires to crumble. Experience is heaped on us in spadefuls like the final earth on a coffin in its damp grave. In short, two or three years after my arrival it was as if I had never lived anywhere else. There was nothing but the pliable present, on which we struggle to impose our valiant but feeble lucidity, and a future which promised not novelty but more of the same. Thus my sense of strangeness was accompanied by indifference not surprise. In that wild place, following the ebb and flow of the seasons, my body, mere substance, with neither destiny nor memory to call its own, was carried along by the recollection in slow motion, until the day capricious death should choose to snatch me from an existence that was at once familiar and strange. My life could no longer consciously conceive of any other possibilities.

Generally speaking it is that which you least expect that happens. One afternoon, some Indians came to my hut in a state of high excitement. In recent days I had been aware of them talking together in low voices and giving me what they imagined to be furtive glances. But they had behaved like that on other occasions: for example, whenever they were preparing themselves to invite me to do something or to help them with some particular task. They had held similar meetings the first time they had taken me hunting with them, or once when a storm threatened and they needed my help in digging up their crops. What made this occasion different was that their attentions, which familiarity had long since helped diminish, suddenly took on a renewed and unexpected intensity.

When I went outside I was greeted by the noise and clamour usually reserved for special days. The whole tribe was gathered outside my hut. Three or four men led me forward, pushing me (not with any intention of harming me, but just in order to hurry me up) or even prodding me for no other reason than that they too were in the grip of an almost uncontrollable excitement. With some difficulty they managed to escort me down to the beach through the jostling crowd who were eager to get near me. Everyone was touching and shaking and even caressing me. They wanted to hold me back but, above all, to attract my attention. Again they adopted those exaggerated poses belied by their pleading, defeated gaze. Indeed their gaze, in which their last remaining hopes seemed to be concentrated, is the most enduring image I retain of them and the final proof too of the persistence of the thing they were trying to conquer or

conceal beneath their unnatural behaviour. In a way it is
the presence of that inexpressible something in their
eyes which drives me on to keep writing in this silent
night. It was always there. I have never seen anyone
drown in a swamp but I think there must be the same
look in the eyes of the man being sucked into the slimy
pit, stripped even of the possibility of struggle which
would only be to co-operate with the very force that is
swallowing him alive. That look, which so many men
have learned to hide, is like the reverse side of a coin, a
constant affront to the deceptively proud carnality of the
visible world. It shows that compassion, though justified,
is useless; with discreet horror it lays bare the vanity of
appearance. Despite, or perhaps because of, its dull
shine, its lustre dimmed by its own obsessions, it has all
the burning clarity of the noonday sun. Accustomed to
reflecting its own dark origins, it brings enlightenment.
Anyone seeing that desperately insistent gaze, anyone
who, despite all efforts to hide it, grasps its meaning may
rightly believe they have understood the price this world
exacts.

Bobbing at the river's edge was the canoe they had
prepared and loaded with food as they had done for my
predecessors. Torn between making way for me and
forcing me to notice them, the Indians were a mass of
contradictory gestures that only increased the noisy
disorder of the crowd. Lifted up by strong, anxious arms,
my feet barely touched the ground over the last few
yards so that I found myself seated at last in the canoe as
if transported there by magic. Almost simultaneously,
several Indians waded into the water and began pushing
the canoe downriver. I sat quite still, not even touching
the paddle, just letting them push me. As I moved off I
looked back at the crowd of Indians clustered together on

the beach. Those nearest the canoe were by now almost waist-deep in the water and seemed to me the last small islands of a troubled continent reaching out into the ocean. Waving, many of them ran downriver along the shore. One dived in and tried to swim alongside. Every two or three strokes he would stop and emerge from the water, gesturing wildly at me and beating his chest only to plunge in again and swim on. Finally I took hold of the paddle and began to steer. As I floated downstream, the scene being enacted before my eyes began to make more sense to me, not less. For the first time the whole tribe, shaken by that ambivalent excitement, became something I could view from the outside. This was especially true of the man swimming alongside me or the Indians running along the shore in the hope that I would notice them, recognize and hold them in my memory for longer than the others and keep their image fresher in my mind. Paradoxically, by the very fact of their having separated from the tribe, they became more blurred to me. Of course I do remember them as individuals as: 'the one who swam alongside the canoe' and 'the ones who ran along the shore', but I cannot be absolutely certain that that was how they wished to be remembered. At last they too fell away. The swimmer made his way to the shore, dripping water, exhausted by the effort; the others ran on a little further, then stood still. I could no longer hear the cries of *Def-ghi! def-ghi!* which they had kept up right until the last moment and scarcely anyone now was waving or making signs or performing other ludicrous actions to make themselves stand out from the anonymity of the crowd. I could see them more clearly than the huts which were just visible through the leaves. They were standing as if frozen against the semicircle of trees that bordered the beach, their faces turned to the river in which the advancing canoe made scarcely a ripple, beneath the solitary sun now setting in a green sky over the pale, yellow earth. As I moved downstream towards an unknown destiny, I felt something which I can only dare to formulate, albeit hesitantly, tonight, sixty years later, now that only the briefest of futures is left to me: no one came down that river in that canoe, no one existed nor had ever existed apart from that person who for ten years had wandered lost and confused in that arena. A bend in the river abruptly erased the vision and I woke from that dream for ever.

The current carried me steadily on until evening and it did not prove too difficult to steer the canoe. For hours I heard nothing but the splash of the paddle in the water and the occasional raucous chatter of birds disturbed by the noise I made when I went too near the shore. Drowsy alligators slid silently down the mud of the crumbling shoreline to the water. Occasionally a fish jumped trying to snap up some tiny morsel. But it was usually only high enough to break the surface so that rather than actually seeing it, I guessed it was there by the noise it made, loud or quiet according to its size, and by the plume of whitish water it left behind. I saw yellow fish that seemed clad in gold; there were some striped like tigers or coppery green with heads like cats or serpents; others I saw were twice the length of a man, as big as cows – in fact all the mysterious, rich diversity of life that had made the river its home. Still keeping the little light burning inside me like a candle flame able to resist any wind, I drifted lost and alone in this world of pure exteriority, amongst an animal ferment of insects, birds, fish, beasts and even monsters. Night fell. It was a pitch-black, moonless night with many stars. The land there is so flat and the horizon is so low and the river so perfectly reflects the sky, that for a long time I seemed to be moving not through water but through the black sky itself. Every time the paddle touched the water the hundreds of stars mirrored in its surface seemed to explode and be blown to dust, seemed to disappear into the element that both gave them origin and fixed them in their place. They changed from steady points of light into shapeless blobs or capricious lines so that it seemed as I passed that the very element through which I drifted was being destroyed and reabsorbed into the dark.

Weariness drove me to the river bank and I slept in the canoe. At dawn, I was woken by a voice saying cautiously, very close by: 'He's got a beard.' When I opened my eyes, two bearded men holding firearms were leaning over me, watching me, surprised. Their heads were crowned with gleaming helmets; they looked tired and a bit simple. They startled me at first as I was sleeping with my head towards the bank and as they bent over me their faces appeared upside down. Waking from a dream, I thought they must be some kind of aborigine whose heads nature had capriciously placed the wrong way up. I sat up with a start, frightening the two men, who stepped back raising their weapons threateningly. I then saw that their heads were in fact in their proper place and that the rather stunned faces staring at me were like many others I had seen as a child in the ports. To calm them I started to tell them my story, but as I talked I saw the look of astonishment grow on their faces until I eventually realized that I was talking to them in the language of the Indians. I tried to speak to them in my mother tongue but found I had forgotten it. At last, with great difficulty, I managed to utter a few isolated words, linking them out of habit in the idiosyncratic syntax of the Indians. Although this did not really help to explain anything, it did at least, given my physical appearance, provide the two men with proof that I too was a stranger in that nightmarish place.

They ordered me to follow them. There was an encampment a short distance downstream, by the shore, and a little further on a ship lay anchored in midriver. In the late dawn everything had taken on that singular colour which, amongst the Indians, would have signalled a day of frenzy and withdrawal. The men's beards were like stiff masks framing their pale, slightly anxious faces. The difficulty we had in communicating brought home to me the fact that after ten years amongst the Indians I no longer knew how to behave towards these men. When we reached the encampment, they hustled me away from the curious eyes of the common soldiers working on the shore and took me to an officer who began interrogating me. Despite my best efforts, I understood very little. He spoke slowly in order to facilitate my understanding, but his words were just so much noise to me: the few isolated sounds which did evoke a precise image were like the almost identifiable fragments of a once-familiar object which lies shattered by some cataclysm. For my part, the few words of our common language which I was able to formulate emerged into each silence that the officer left for my replies as if enmeshed in the webs and nets of words I had learned amongst the Indians and which, like the native plants of the region, proved the stronger, faster growing, more flourishing and abundant species. Finally, we ended up using sign language to communicate: yes, there were Indians less than a day's journey upriver; it might take longer to get there travelling against the current; they called themselves *colastiné*; no, they did not have any gold or precious stones, but they did have lances, bows and arrows; and, yes, they did eat human flesh. The officer shook his head somewhat impatiently. Although, as I found out later, this was the first time he had set foot in that land, he found confirmation of his own suspicions and opinions in each of my rudimentary replies and took each of the Indians' characteristics, however innocent, as a personal affront. I had the feeling that even I seemed suspect to him, as if my long sojourn in that land had contaminated me with some negative aura. He was on the point of throwing me in the dungeons but at the last moment he agreed to have me put in the hands of a priest. The officer was what in this part of the world people would call a handsome fellow: his hair and beard were black, the hair straight and the beard well-trimmed, he had an athletic and well-proportioned body and his skin looked tanned and healthy from long exposure to sea and harsh weather. Even in that remarkable dawn, on the muddy shore from which crocodiles, spiders and natives watched with feigned indifference, he seemed — erect, sleek and elegant in his starched shirt and glinting metal – like someone dressed for a regal ball. When he felt he had gleaned sufficient information he appeared to forget all about me and began issuing orders which were quickly and faithfully carried out by his subalterns. During the few days I was able to observe him I realized how much both soldiers and sailors respected him. His dry, laconic jokes helped to alleviate the backbreaking work of all those under his command, as if he were aware of the privileges command brought with it and felt compassion and even some kind of love for his men, though I, from the very first time I saw him, felt a kind of revulsion which only increased in the days that followed. Taking me with them, the men hurried back to the ship anchored in the river and for the next two hours, with a great show of arms and much shouting, they prepared themselves for an expedition. The ship sailed on upriver until nightfall and then dropped anchor far from the shore. I found a corner of the deck where I could spend the night, attended by the priest who, between long periods of silence, interrogated me gently but without success: either I was just too tired or the events were too vague and distant for my senses to find, somewhere in the depths of my being, a language to express them. The next morning the officer interrogated me again, pointing to the shores of the river. I used my hands to help explain to him that the village was not far away. From where we stood near the gunwale I saw that another ship had anchored near ours during the night. Several small boats of armed men had disembarked from this ship and were approaching ours, where the crew were also preparing themselves. Right up until the last moment the officer seemed intent on taking me with him on this expedition, but a distrust of my person, which came perhaps from an intuition of the revulsion he inspired in me, led him not only to leave me on board but to have me sent to the hold with the priest, as if he suspected I might betray them or place a curse on them. I should say that, from the first, the curiosity I and my adventures aroused was mingled with feelings of suspicion and rejection. It was as if my contact with that savage world had infected me with some contagious disease, and the very fact of having been kept for so long away from the world to which the men belonged meant I had returned contaminated by what lay beyond it

The expedition set out at mid-morning and returned at nightfall; they had found the trees, the semi-circle of beach and the village but the only sign of its supposed inhabitants was some still warm ashes mixed with the sandy earth. Accompanied by the priest, I was sent for by the officer to be interrogated for a third time. At his request I explained as best I could in weary gestures and fragmented sentences which confused words from the two languages with others which were a mixture of both and incomprehensible in either. I told him that the Indians had no doubt seen the ships coming and had retreated to the interior, as I had often seen them do in times of flood or when threatened by invasion by a neighbouring tribe. As if he had foreseen just such an affront, the officer nodded solemnly, half-closing his eyes. His gestures seemed to indicate his conviction that, out of who knows what sense of duty or obligation, the Indians should have stayed and waited instead of retreating to the interior when they saw the shiploads of armed soldiers approaching. He was arrogant enough to assume that somehow the Indians should have known about his plans for them beforehand, approved of them without hesitation and then done everything they could to facilitate their execution. It was inconceivable to him that the Indians might have a response of their own to those plans.

After they had exhausted me with further pointlessly repeated questionings, they transferred me and my priest to the other ship. Left in the charge of different officers, I was interrogated again under the curious gaze of the sailors and at last relegated to a corner of the deck. To the clothes I had been given that first day to hide my genitals, they added a shirt and a pair of trousers which at first I just could not get on with. I felt strange and alienated from my body in the scratchy clothes, but gradually I forgot I had them on and got used to wearing them. The next morning the priest woke me up to cut my beard and hair and give me something to eat. Through him I learned that a new expedition had left at dawn for the coast, at which time our ship had set sail downriver. I leaned over the rail. I could see nothing but the silent, empty shore and the great wild river flowing down to the sea. Even though only a short time had elapsed since we set off, there was no sign of either Indians or soldiers. We dropped anchor as night fell. The overwhelming silence which came from the shores we had been slowly leaving behind us grew oppressive. I studied the watery horizon though without quite knowing why. Returned from its periodic absence, the moon rose that night like a thin yellow arc. From the mosquito-infested deck, I stared up through the masts and ropes at the innumerable stars. Not a sound rose up to them; and from upriver not even a murmur disturbed the sleeping deck, there was only the same uninterrupted silence that had reigned throughout the day.

The next day was the same. At dawn we continued downriver and at night dropped anchor. The crew showed no interest whatsoever in the ship we had left behind amongst the flat, forgotten islands. I was the only one looking anxiously back beyond the wake of the ship. With the dawn of the third day the sought-after signs appeared. Unlike us the dead had not stopped for the night and many had overtaken us and were floating ahead of the prow. Although there were quite a few soldiers among the bodies, they were mostly Indians: men, women, old people and children. Many of the soldiers were pierced through the chest or throat by a single arrow I ran to the stern and found that to both port and starboard we were surrounded by a multitude of corpses floating downriver almost as fast as the ship so that for the next two or three days the ship continued on its way escorted by a host of bodies. When a drowned and sleeping face turned towards them, the sailors would give it a name, pleased to be able to recognize the soldier to whom it belonged. But the officers gave orders that the corpses were not to be lifted out of the water. Stiffened and blurred by death, Indians and soldiers alike formed a silent procession that moved ever faster until the river reached the widest part of its estuary and opened out into the same sweet sea the captain had discovered ten years before. The corpses dispersed and were lost to the vast, welcoming ocean. That same day I learned that the ship was to cross those waters – a monotonous bridge of days stretching out beneath a blazing sun – to what the sailors with pompous solemnity called 'our homeland'.

Day by day the language of my childhood, of which in those first moments only indecipherable fragments had seemed to survive, began to come slowly back to me until it was as whole and intimate as before. First it returned to my memory, then I felt the rhythm of it in my veins. The priest's persistence in this helped me, but though he performed his charitable duties conscientiously enough, he was more suspicious of me than anyone; I could tell by the slant his questions took that he was convinced my stay with the Indians, about whom he knew nothing, had been an opportunity for me to partake of every sin. Though he looked after me for three or four months until, to his great relief, he was able to deliver me into good hands, he clearly viewed prolonged close contact with me as tantamount to keeping company with the Devil. Had it not been for his sense of duty and his scrupulous attention to his ecclesiastical obligations, he would gladly have abandoned me, for it was evident that I inspired in him more fear than compassion. The distrust I aroused was stronger in the priest than in anyone else: he would certainly have been more at ease with me had I been a leper. This deep-seated suspicion of me was at first so widespread that I even wondered at times if my very survival and long acquaintance with the Indians constituted some secret crime which any honourable man would have felt guilty about, or if the Indians, without my realizing, had made me so much a part of their rich essence that I bore some sign of this which was obvious to everyone except me. Interrogated again and again both during the voyage and on my arrival, I was the constant object of veiled glances and probing looks from men trying to extract from me information about matters with which they were obsessed and of which I was ignorant. Officers, civil servants, sailors and priests alike seemed gripped by the same obsession which, like me, they knew absolutely nothing about. And neither they nor I could decide whether their persistent and baseless suspicions about me were justified or not.

Only one man seemed immune from those suspicions, not so much because he pitied me but because he was too wise to take them seriously. That man, Father Quesada, died more than forty years ago. The priest who had accompanied me on the boat and who had brought me here like someone carrying a live coal in the palm of his hand, worried more for his own salvation than for mine and convinced by his own credulity that the two were linked, began to feel that the time had come to get rid of me. And so, once I had been interrogated, studied and bustled hither and thither by learned men and courtiers, he suggested to some people in positions of power that the only possible destiny for me was the Church. Thanks to that priest's belief in my bedevilment, I met Father Quesada. I spent seven years with him in a monastery

from which one could see a small white village perched
on a hill.

Many months had passed from the day the soldiers
had found me asleep in the canoe at dawn and that late
afternoon when, under guard, I reached the monastery
on horseback. During that time I had sunk deep into
sadness, as into a pool of murky water Words turned to
fistfuls of ash in my mouth and in the indifferent light of
day everything seemed utterly bleak. The temptation
not to move or speak grew in me daily, as did the desire
just to let myself vegetate in a corner. During that period
my eyes would fill with tears at the sight of a leaf falling,
or a certain street in the port or the folds of a garment, or
at the least insignificant thing At times I could feel that
something inside me was dwindling almost to vanishing
point and then the world, beginning with my own body,
would seem like some strange, far-off object devoid of
meaning, which emitted only a monotonous buzzing.
When not besieged by these extremes of feeling, I spent
the days as if in a dream, insensible to the depth or
texture of things, impoverished by apathy. Within
months I began to find the slightest gesture or movement difficult. I would spend many hours standing in
front of a window, seeing neither the glass nor what lay
beyond it. My first wish when I woke in the morning was
for night to come so that I might lay myself down to sleep
again. When they were not hauling me off here, there
and everywhere to be questioned or observed, I would lie
the whole day in my rickety bed, half-awake, my mind a
blank It was as if, and now is the the first time I am
aware of this, I was asking to be rescued by oblivion from
something that was burying me beneath ever denser
layers of grief and pain that had no cause.

Father Quesada managed to wrest me from my misery simply by his presence. He was not just a good man, he was brave and intelligent too and, when he was in the mood, he could keep me laughing for hours. The other members of the community pretended to disapprove of him but deep down they envied him. He was fifty years old when I met him. He had a grey, tangled beard, thinning hair that made him look a little older than he was, but his body was sturdy and muscular, his head set firmly on his shoulders. His veins, muscles and skin, burned dark by the sun, had the look of roots, or dried, twisted wood. The first time I saw him he was returning to the monastery on horseback. I remember that I heard the horse's hooves before I saw the rider and that what made me turn round was the slightly censorious look given him by the monk who was letting us in. His tangle of grey, silky hair was silhouetted against the setting sun and the sweat ran in grubby trails from his forehead and cheekbones into his beard. He emanated a resigned, generous insolence. I knew, from the one rapid glance he gave me, that he understood my troubles, found them justified and pitied them. And yet he was smiling, almost ironically, as if he had seen into my own mystery more clearly than I myself and, thanks to his insight, had reduced my suffering to tolerable dimensions. That ironical look which so irritated his peers had the invulnerability of metal long tempered in the fire but never destroyed by it. The only reason one could have for describing him as less than human was that he knew nothing of the errant disquiet of panic, or of resigned distraction. That first encounter, though it lasted only a few seconds, gave me not so much courage or lucidity as some slight, confused sense of hope. Father Quesada nodded a greeting to us and headed his horse in the direction of the stables.

He was an erudite, even wise man and everything that can be taught I learned from him. In him I had at last found a father and he slowly dragged me out of the grey abyss into which I had fallen and, by stages, won for me the most this world has to offer: a neutral, stable, monotone state of mind, equidistant between enthusiasm and indifference, which, every now and then, finds its justification in the experience of some brief elation. It was not easy. Teaching me Latin, Greek, Hebrew and science was the least of it: what he found hard was convincing me of their value and importance. For him they were tools which could be used to grasp and manipulate the incandescent world of the senses; for me, fascinated as I was by the contingent, it was like going out to hunt a beast that had already devoured me. And yet he did improve me. It took him years and my efforts were sustained more by my love of his patience and simplicity than by any love of knowledge. Later, much later, years after his death, I understood that if Father Quesada had not taught me to read and write, the one act which might justify my life would have been beyond my reach.

I recall that I did not see him again during my first days there and later learned that he had travelled to Córdoba and Seville for discussions with friends and in search of some treatise or other. His learning brought him freedoms that the other members of the community thought excessive, but because he was consulted by so many eminent people, they had to put up with it.

On horseback he had seemed a tall man, but when I saw him again, walking in one of the cloisters, I realized that he was in fact rather short. It was, however, the very smallness of his body that seemed to concentrate, even emphasize his strength, an intelligent strength which eschewed ostentation and thus violence. It was perhaps not so much strength as firmness, a quality which, despite his modesty or even his fits of pride, he used less to convince or transform than to maintain his own impassivity. His own peculiar brand of humility took the form of using self-deprecating remarks to make fun of himself. These were applauded more warmly by his enemies than by those who loved him, the former doubtless hoping to have their calumnies confirmed by reality. The loud excess of vulgar laughter with which they greeted the caricature Father Quesada presented of himself was audible proof of their hatred and he, aware of this, continued to play the fool for them out of pure charity. He pretended not to notice how much this distressed the few people in the monastery who did love him, as if demanding of them the same humility. Though I would never have dared to question his behaviour, as a newcomer, seeing the situation from an outsider's point of view, I could not judge to what extent his attitude was a calculated one. For as I gradually got to know the other monks, I realized that beneath their pious, kindly exterior many of them (having authority on their side) would be capable of committing the most heinous of crimes. No doubt seeing them for what they were, namely ignorant, superstitious, mean-spirited, opportunistic, pettifogging and childish, Father Quesada put his pride to one side so as not to hurt them. However, it was also a means of protecting himself because, in spite of their mild and gentle manners, they had it in their power to have a man sent to the stake. As far as religion was concerned, Father Quesada doubtless had his faults, but then so did the others, without, in compensation, possessing any of his virtues It was said that he made his frequent visits to Córdoba and Seville in order to visit his concubines, a rumour which, apart from being a matter of complete indifference to me, I never had occasion to verify. He was certainly an uninhibited lover of wine but this, far from corrupting him, seemed to me only to improve him. The qualities which, out of humility, he concealed when sober, blazed forth once he had drunk a little wine in the company of friends and, without his realizing it, made him even more deserving of our love. For whole nights he would keep us dazzled and amused on every subject under the sun. He was a fine, open-minded philosopher, a patient, exacting thinker as fascinated by everyday life as he was by physics or theology. When he really had drunk too much, he would grow sad, but it was a compassionate sadness for the fate of others: not once in seven years did I hear him bemoan his own lot. In those dawns that brought not a breath of cool air, he would fall silent, sweating a little from the quantity of wine he had drunk, and stare unblinking into space. Then suddenly, shaking his head, he would begin to talk, for example, of Simon the Cyrenian, pitying the cruel fate that had placed him on the road of the cross and forced him to be an instrument in Christ's Calvary; or he would talk about St Peter in tears after thrice denying Christ. At that point, his friends would smile knowingly at one another and start to say their farewells secure in the knowledge that within five minutes the father would be snoring in his armchair. I would get him up out of his chair and lead him, docile and distracted, his hand resting on my shoulder, to his cell: he would be asleep, stretched out on his bed, before I had closed the door behind me. His liking for wine grew with the years and his meetings with his friends which, when I first met him, had taken place monthly, were later held once, twice, even three times a week. The father claimed he suffered from terrible back pains that only wine could ease. In the last few months of his life, however, he drank nothing, and to this day I wonder if it was not that that killed him. What I do know is that he went out riding early one morning and a few hours later his horse returned riderless; he was dead when we found him at nightfall amongst the desolate mountains. He had no visible wound apart from a little trickle of blood from his nose which had already dried on his white beard. We never knew if it was the fall or an attack that had killed him. As it was high summer he must have lain dying beneath the open sky, with his face turned towards the same intense, enigmatic light that his intelligence had confronted all the days of his life.

It was pity, not curiosity, that made him take such trouble over me, although as he got to know me he did become increasingly interested in my 'case', as he sometimes called my odd situation. I should perhaps mention that the deaths of the captain and my companions had been observed by the great majority of the crew who had remained on board the ships. On their return to port, the story had been told in every large town and for months it was discussed, amplified, distorted and tirelessly touted around from the port cities to the courts and from there to the big commercial centres. Several similar cases had been reported in various places in Africa and the Indies. In one such case, some Indians had kidnapped a group of sailors, and after much deliberation the rest of the crew, instead of withdrawing, had decided to go to their companions' rescue. However, when they reached the village they discovered that the Indians had eaten their prisoners raw leaving only a scattering of gristly bones and scalped heads. The human condition of the Indians was the subject of much dispute. Some did not even consider them to be men; others thought that though they might be men they were certainly not Christian men; and most thought that if they were not Christians they could not be men. From time to time during my lessons Father Quesada would ask me disconcerting questions and note down the answers, often making me repeat them in order to glean further details. Did they have a form of government? Did they own property? How and where did they defecate? Did they barter hand-crafted objects with neighbouring tribes? Were they musical? Did they have a religion? Did they wear jewellery on their arms, in their nose, round their neck, in their ears or any other part of their body? With which hand did they eat? With the information he gathered, Father Quesada wrote a very brief treatise which he entitled *An account of the adventures of a child lost to the world* in which he set down our dialogues. I should say, however, that at the time I was still stunned by what had happened to me, and my respect for Father Quesada was so great that I felt too intimidated to speak to him of many essential things his questions failed to elicit. I remember that once, during one of his meetings with his friends, he smiled and shook his head and I heard him say that the Indians were sons of Adam, doubtless unacknowledged, but sons of Adam for all that and therefore they were men like us. I clearly remember thinking to myself that night that for me the Indians were the only men on this earth, and that since the day they had sent me back, with the exception of Father Quesada I had met only strange, problematic beings whom only custom or convention dignified with the name of 'man'.

The monastery, which should have been a place of retreat, was the scene of endless comings and goings. The monks from good families had their own servants, and people from outside came and went at all hours: relatives, visitors, peasants, artisans, sellers, and often monks who were passing through the region spent the night there. Each monk would receive his friends, protectors and even, in more than one case, his mistresses. The novices were made the errand boys of those who had already been ordained. Religious festivals would begin with early morning mass and be spread out over one or two days with all kinds of entertainments and feasts. Now and then the superior would call the fathers together and urge discretion on them. But he himself, having a large number of relatives in high places, spent his days receiving artists and people of influence and organizing processions and poetry contests in honour of some saint or other, in the hope they would surpass in brilliance those held in other nearby monasteries. Once a Court painter came to stay with us in order to paint a Last Supper for the refectory. He stayed nearly a year and caused a great stir with all his preliminary preparations. He studied us all closely, full face and in profile, had us show him our hands and take up the strangest poses, then dressed us up in all kinds of different costumes. At last he chose his models and set to work. The whole monastery was placed at his disposal; he ordered everyone around, including the Superior, who was so delighted to have him there that he meekly and respectfully indulged the artist's every whim. The painter was always demanding that things be found for him that minute and if you passed the door of the room where he was painting, he could still be heard loudly issuing orders. But sometimes, when the day was nearly done and the light was beginning to fade, he would dismiss his models with a weary, distracted air, put away his materials with meticulous care and then, with a bottle of wine concealed beneath his cloak, he would make for Father Quesada's booklined cell where he would stay until long after midnight engaged in calm, civilized conversation.

It was only Father Quesada's presence that kept me at the monastery. Had it been up to me I would not have stayed so long. I was used to harsh weather, to real silence and to solitude. All the bustle in the monastery made me dizzy. Moreover the father had guessed that, as far as I was concerned, the religion that was intended to bring about my regeneration was no more to me than the monotonous mumbling of senseless words and the ritual repetition of empty gestures. In my first days there, before the father took charge of me, they had placed me in the hands of an exorcist who was to free me of my demons with his Latin formulae. After several weeks of this, Father Quesada intervened and got them to leave me in peace. I began to serve him at table and to tidy his cell and, little by little, he set about teaching me to read and write. Seeing the rapid progress I made, he decided to tell me about other things too because, as he put it, I was like a naked newborn babe just delivered from my mother's womb. I rarely spoke and he respected my silence. He said to me once, shortly before he died, that there are two types of suffering: in the first the sufferer knows he is suffering and is aware that while he suffers a better life, whose taste still lingers in his memory, is being slowly conjured away from him; in the second the sufferer is unaware that he suffers but to that person the world, even in its humblest manifestations, seems a scorched and deserted place as he passes through it The exorcists could try if they liked to drive out with their Latin phrases this unacknowledged suffering, Father Quesada said, his eyes averted, no doubt afraid that my face might involuntarily betray the presence of just such suffering in me, but the truth was that nothing could plumb its depths and only the destruction of the world itself could finally and completely eradicate it.

This fine man, who had never given an inch in his head-on confrontation with the truth, was brought back to the monastery one summer night, silent and inert, a trickle of blood staining his white beard. As far as I am concerned, 'father' is exactly the word for him – that is what he was to me, coming as I do from nothingness and returning as I am slowly and fearlessly through successive births to the common place of origin. No sooner had the earth closed over him than I gathered together my few possessions, got on my horse and went off to lose myself for a while in the cities.

The first years were years of shadow and ashes. Like a man half-dead, I wandered through an indiscriminate jumble of worlds, or rather through mere husks of worlds. I drifted through bloodless lands together with other insubstantial detritus who clung miraculously to a vague semblance of humanity. And it was surely only by some miracle that I survived. Most days I obtained food by begging or rooting around in piles of rubbish. Occasionally I found some lowly temporary job. Obviously times were hard and my way of life bore little resemblance to that of other men, but it is also true to say that, still during those years, my abrupt re-entry into the world had left me in a state of shock and any reason or desire I might have had to go on living was almost non-existent. Until then, being and living had been one and the same thing and to go on living had been for me like a steady, uninterrupted flow of water, however bitter. Since my return, living had become something that happened outside myself, something whose incomprehensible, fragile evolution I watched unfold from a distance and which I knew the slightest jolt could bring crashing down. It was as if my very life had been driven out from my own being and because of that had come to seem dark and superfluous. Sometimes I felt less than nothing – if by 'feeling nothing' we understand a state of animal calm and resignation. To feel less than nothing is to exist in a state of abandoned, lingering, viscous chaos, where language is mere babble. Precisely because one feels less than nothing and is even free of the alien power of desire, one struggles on in an impenetrable, blind limbo of self-hatred and dreams of annihilation.

However, in the least likely of places an unexpected peace awaited me. One night in an inn, a group of people eating and getting drunk at the next table to mine got talking with me once their meal was over – I no longer remember how. There were two men – one old and one young – and four women. Realizing that I was a person of some learning they took me for a man of letters and I, in turn, learned that they were actors. The wine drew us closer. They travelled from village to village and town to town putting on plays and scraped a living from that childish employment. The old man limped slightly but had, despite his poverty, a certain dignity. He was intelligent and not immune to the pleasures of conversation. When he realized that I knew Latin and Greek and had some knowledge of both Terence and Plautus, he proposed that I join them to share what dangers and profits came their way. The young man, his nephew, addressed all the women as 'cousin'. Without revealing that for me it was a choice between a life in the theatre and one spent scavenging rubbish dumps, and encouraged by the night's wine, I accepted his proposal.

And so it was that we set off along the highways. From the covered wagon I watched olive groves, wheatfields and bare expanses of rocky ground go by. The empty fields sometimes reminded me of the one great experience of my past life. One day, on one of those hot spring afternoons that exude pleasure, we were camping amongst some trees near a stream. While the others were sleeping or strolling around, I told my story to the old man. He listened half-pitying and half-amazed, and when I had finished began talking excitedly in a low, feverish voice, moving closer to me and looking cautiously around him from time to time. It was as though he were afraid that his proposal, which he guarded as if it were a cache of buried treasure, might be heard by unknown spies eager to profit from his plans. What had happened to me all those years ago was, he told me, known throughout the continent and had become a legend through the constant retelling of it. If our company were to create and put on a play based on those events, our fortunes were assured. Leaning confidentially towards me, the old man, his unblinking eyes half-closed, awaited my reply. I knew all too well how preposterous our 'art' was, how self-interested and vulgar our aims. But indifference is often the secret driving force behind the most successful of enterprises and though in some of their dealings the company at times verged on the criminal, they had proved loyal and friendly to me and so I agreed to write a play for them and to appear in it playing myself.

It was not hard. I simply left all truth out of the verses I wrote and if the odd scrap slipped through by mistake, the old man would make me cross it out, less concerned with the exact details of my experience than with his audience's expectations. When it was written, he gathered the company together for me to read it to them. After I had finished, my select audience, who had put on their sternest and most intelligent expressions to listen, crowded round me, congratulating me on the prosodic perfection of my verses and the mathematical precision of the plot. We began to rehearse: the old man played the part of the captain, his nephew the rest of my companions, and the women the savages. Naturally I was to play the one role that was left unfilled, myself.

And then the performances began. After the opening night, our reputation preceded us. We became so famous that we were even summoned to Court and applauded by the King. I was astonished. When I saw the audiences' enthusiasm for the play, I kept wondering if, without my knowing it, it was not transmitting some secret message which proved as vital to men as the air they breathed. Or perhaps during the performances, we actors played our parts unaware that the audience were also playing theirs; perhaps we were all characters in a play of which my play was nothing but an obscure detail and whose plot escaped us, a plot mysterious enough for our commonplace baseness and empty actions to pass for essential truths. Long, long ago the true meaning of our cheap parody must already have been written into some grander plot that also encompassed us; otherwise all the applause and honours we amassed during our tour, all the parties and the gold lavished on us were undeserved rewards. The kings who came to be entertained by our play must have seen something in it we did not; how else could one explain the absurdity of the secret orders given to their treasurers to reward us so munificently? I sailed, unmoved, through this uncertain hour of triumph. My colleagues were less restrained. They revelled in it all with the perfect, exuberant innocence of the storyteller who, more out of ignorance than charity, reveals the acceptable face of things to an audience of scarecrows labouring under the illusion that they are sensitive lovers of truth. The generous payment they received seemed irrefutable proof to my companions that everything was as it should be in a just and well-ordered world. We lived off that misapprehension for years. The most surprising part is that in all that time not one sensible voice was raised to denounce the play for what it was. In the midst of the constant congratulatory clamour that greeted us I expected at any moment to hear the sceptical, reproving silence that would expose our fraud once and for all. Eventually, however, I realized that the silence I was waiting for had existed in me from the first and that its very presence amidst the unreasoning bustle of courts and cities reduced crowds to the condition of lifeless puppets, mere phantasmagoria in fact. Thanks to those empty vessels calling themselves men I learned the bitter, somewhat superior laugh of one who has the advantage of experience when it comes to the art of generalities. The success of our play told me more about the true essence of my fellow man than all the atrocities perpetrated by armies, or the obscene plunderings of commerce, or the moral juggling that goes on in order to justify every kind of evil. The wild applause that greeted my foolish verses was proof of the absolute vacuity of those people, and at every performance I felt as if I were standing before a crowd of straw men in faded clothes, or insubstantial forms inflated by the indifferent air of the planet. Sometimes I would deliberately garble the meaning of my own speeches and deliver absurd and empty perorations in the hope of getting some reaction from the audience. I wanted to force the audience to realize it was all a fraud, but my stratagems made not a jot of difference to their response. Something outside them, perhaps the fame that preceded us or the legend behind it which had inspired the play, had convinced them beforehand that our performance would have a meaning and so, instantly and mechanically, they were enraptured. There began to be a demand for us in other countries on the continent where other languages were spoken and, one night, in order to make ourselves universally understood, the old man and I transformed the play into a mime. Someone would deliver a prologue in the local language explaining the main events of the play and we would then come on stage to act them out. The absence of words made the play even thinner, for in mime it was reduced to a dry, skimpy skeleton from which hung not a single shred, however bloodless, of real life. All that remained was music, colour and a few acrobatics thrown in to give the ghosts watching our arbitrary gestures the illusion of being in the presence of real intensity and meaning. Our triumph spread through-out the continent, even to the darkest and coldest of courts. Indifferent to it all, I nevertheless allowed myself to be drawn into a way of life I could not fathom.

We acquired wealth and worldliness. The old man and his nephew began to dress like gentlemen. I just let my earnings pile up without quite knowing what to do with it all. Not satisfied with appearing on stage dressed as they imagined Indians would dress, the women went whoring; they spent any free time they had warming the beds of sundry noblemen. We no longer camped out in our wagons but stayed in inns. We were received in castles and in monasteries. Wise men and government officers often came to interview me. I had learned from the old man that it is always best to give people the answers they expect to hear. After our meetings, my interrogators would once more retreat to breathe the cosy atmosphere of their own beliefs, glad to have had their convictions confirmed by external evidence. I spent my time alone, smiling a silent, bitter smile which, with the years, became a habitual scowl.

Over five or six years, one of the women, the last and youngest to have joined us, gave birth to three children, the fruit of her mercenary couplings. No sooner had they begun to walk than the old man had them up on stage acting the part of savages. Their plight touched me and I grew fond of them. The two boys and a girl all had different fathers, which was tantamount to saying that, like me, they had none. The old man who, like his nephew, had no doubt participated in the fertilization process, would look at them from time to time, make some comment on the life their mother led, and shake his head pityingly. In my free time I taught them to read and write. Docile and adrift in the world, they grew more and more attached to me. After a performance one night, the mother went off with a man and never returned. A jealous lover had stabbed her repeatedly and abandoned her by the roadside. It seems it had been raining since dawn and the water had washed away the blood; in her white skin made livid by the murderous blows and the rain, her wounds looked like old scars revealed at last by death.

After a performance one night I felt so sickened by the falseness of it all that I decided to leave the troupe. Concern for the children had something to do with my decision too. Although the old man was as weary of it all as I was and much closer to death, he would not hear of my leaving, convinced that without me the play's success would be greatly diminished. He was not entirely wrong.

There was no doubt that my status as real-life survivor lent the show much of its impact. But it pained him to have to go against my wishes, for he recognized that his business had begun to prosper largely thanks to me and, after years of observing my silent, solitary nature and my steadfast indifference to matters of profit and loss, he had acquired a sneaking respect for me, mingled perhaps with compassion. Leaving him was painful for me too, for I had been useful to him and there was no denying that the actors had unwittingly hauled me up out of a deep well and landed me on the easy, neutral soil of resignation. The old man was also opposed to my taking the children, saying that they were essential members of the company. But he did not insist on it too much, knowing that that was one point I would not compromise on. After hours of discussion, we finally hit on an acceptable solution: his nephew, who was more or less my age, could play my part and even take on my identity. I in turn would change my name and promise never to write another play based on my adventures. Agreement was soon reached. We were staying in the dark and foggy north at the time. One morning, I wrapped the children up in furs and set out along a dank road which bisected two plains. The bluish snow covering the landscape only increased the impression of absence and immateriality. I said goodbye to the old man and the other actors and began the journey south. We travelled for months, almost without stopping, until we reached a white city set amongst vineyards and olive groves beneath the baking sun.

We settled down in that city, in the very house where I am writing. I had accumulated a fair sum of money and, before parting company, the old man had given me a portion of the murdered woman's savings. I had acquired a taste for books from Father Quesada and their silent music often filled the tedium of unending days. In the countries of the north I had learned how books were printed and it occurred to me that I could do the same, not so much to increase my own fortune as to teach a trade to those I now considered to be my children; this would give them something more solid than mere posturings and appearances to hold on to. We did rather well. Work in the printing house was like a game to them and as they grew older my leisure time increased. We are not perhaps the most joyful of people, but we have a highly developed sense of discretion and loyalty. I have grandchildren and great-grandchildren now: at times the printing house resounds to their laughter and during the day the noise drifts up from there to my room. In the last few years my life has been limited to the occasional family gathering, an ever briefer evening stroll and reading. At night, after supper, I light the candle and, with the window wide open to the tranquil starry dark, sit down to remember and to write. After the hubbub in the streets has died away, the summer night fills my white room with the scents of heaven and honeysuckle and, as silence falls on the city, this washes me clean of all the noise of my years. Very occasionally the rain starts to hammer down, and when the first drops fall after many days of heat they strike the parched whitewashed walls and instantly sizzle dry in a puff of white dust. I am accustomed to harsh weather and find the short, temperate winters here easily tolerable. Beyond the window panes the trees form a gleaming filigree of knotted, black branches against a background of dark blue sky. Every night at half past ten, one of my daughters-in-law brings me my supper which is always the same: some bread, a dish of olives, a glass of wine.

Though repeated punctually every night, this remains a special moment. Indeed its nightly repetition, as reliably regular as the movement of the constellations, is the most luminous and benevolent of all its qualities. My room, apart from one wall of books, is almost empty; the table, the chair, the bed and the candlestick holders stand out black against the white walls. The white dish and the gleaming black and green olives only just spooned out from the jar where they are kept in the kitchen; the tall glass full of wine the colour of thin honey which gives off an earthy, pungent aroma— all of these shine in the flickering light of the candle flames which, in the still air, seek to retrieve their proper height and fixity. The coarse bread on its own white plate is irrefutable and dense, and its daily reappearance, along with the wine and olives, is a modest miracle bestowing an aura of eternity. Putting my pen down, I slowly raise the olives one by one to my mouth. I spit the stones out into the hollow of my hand and place them carefully on the side of the plate. When they leave my mouth they are still warm from the heat my body lends them. Out of sheer habit, I alternate green olives with black, and the two tastes, one after the other, always call up for me an image of green and black stripes which passes seamlessly from mouth to memory. My first sip of wine tastes exactly as it did the previous night and on every night before that, and this constancy provides me, now I am an old man, with one of my first certainties. It is so rare and so fragile that it is not in itself a proof of anything. To be honest, it is not so much a certainty as an indication of an impossible truth, an internal order proper to the world and very close to our experience of eternity, which some see as a superior attribute, but which in fact is nothing more than a modest, banal symbol, gawdy imitation jewellery dangled before our meagre senses. It is a luminous moment which, though it occurs every night at suppertime and is gone in an instant, always induces in me a few moments of drowsiness. It is at any rate all in vain, for in the monotonous passing of the days such moments do nothing to check the inexorable night which rules them and which carries us down the road to the slaughter-house. And yet each night it is moments such as these which sustain the hand holding the pen which, in the name of those who are now definitively lost, sets down the signs which tentatively seek to give them enduring life.

I slowly came to realize that nothing could remain of those lost people. As I sailed out to sea on that ship with its escort of corpses, it had been obvious to me that they had been unable to protect themselves when that new storm from the outer world began to batter them. It must be said that they were not people to make war for the sake of it. The only part it played in their lives was in their annual expeditions, from which they would return, prompt and punctilious, with their prisoners. They never provoked war, unless one counts those occasions when neighbouring tribes attacked them in reprisal for the victims seized for their festivals. Their sallies were more hunting expeditions than wars. The Indians were more like hunters than warriors and their expeditions were motivated by necessity and not by the blood lust which lies at the root of all war. Indeed they pitied warlike people and appeared to consider a propensity for war as a kind of illness. They seemed to think of war as senseless waste, the bad habit of irrational children. It was not the bloody nature of war that discomfited them; what aroused their disapproval was the destruction and the domestic upheaval it brought in its wake. When attacked they lamented the disorder left behind, the

burned houses, the broken pots, the lost tools and the
general confusion rather than their wounded or their
dead. They always put up a good fight, making it seem
almost easy; perhaps that is why the attacks against
them were so infrequent. The surrounding tribes must
have been afraid of them or at least had a healthy respect
for them because, in all the years I was there, there were
no more than three or four attacks and only two of those
had been on the village. The other occasions had been
fleeting attacks on the men going out to hunt. On the
whole the aggressors came off worst. The extraordinary
speed of the Indians disoriented and surprised their
attackers, precipitating them into flight, defeat or death.
Now it seems comical the way the Indians would stop in
mid-battle to fling up their arms in extravagant lamenta-
tions over an overturned or broken pot or a roof in
flames and the way they would upbraid their enemies
while poisoned arrows cut the clear air around them.
They seemed far more concerned about damage to
property than about an arrow embedding itself in the
throat of a member of their family. And it was evident
that, the battle over, they paid more attention to their
goods than to their wounded. They gave the disagreeable
impression of being peace-loving purely out of small-
mindedness. They killed off the prisoners and wounded
of the enemy tribe without cruelty but with no pretence
at compassion and stripped them of weapons and
jewellery. Sometimes they cut off their heads, mutilated
them and threw the pieces into the river. After the
battle, their main concern was to clean up and put
everything in order; they would sweep and wash, repair
huts and earthenware pots so that the next day no one
would have known that only a few hours before death,
fire and disorder had laid the village to waste.

It was perhaps that very meticulousness which proved their downfall. It is not unlikely that, after withdrawing inland before the arrival of the soldiers, they had begun to reflect on the state of their houses and their belongings and had returned to rescue or protect them, subordinating the danger of death to that of waste and disorder. In any case death meant nothing to them. Death and life were the same to them, and men, objects and animals, alive or dead, coexisted in the same dimension. They wanted to stay alive as much as anyone but dying was not more terrible to them than other dangers which filled them with genuine panic. As long as it was real, death did not frighten them. I can easily imagine them returning to look for their belongings under a hail of bullets; I am also sure that the escort of livid bodies that days later floated downriver alongside the ships had felt neither fear nor sadness on abandoning this life. It was not the impossibility of the other world that terrified them but the impossibility of this one. The other world formed part of this world; the two were one and the same thing. If this world were real, then the other was too. It only needed one thing to be real for everything else, visible or invisible, to take on reality.

For years after my return from those lands, whenever I was anywhere near a port I would succumb to the temptation of questioning sailors just back from a voyage. My hope was to glean some details from their confused stories which would give me a clue as to the fate of the tribe. But for the sailors all Indians were the same and unlike me they could not distinguish between the different tribes, places and names. They did not know that in an area covering only a few miles there were many different tribes living side by side. Each one was not just a community or the overspill from some nearby group but an autonomous world with its own internal laws; each tribe had its own language, customs and beliefs and lived in a dimension impenetrable to outsiders. It was not only the people who were different: space, time, water, plants, sun, moon and stars were all different too. Each tribe lived in a singular universe, infinite and unique, which bore no relation whatsoever to that of neighbouring tribes. During my time amongst the Indians I gradually learned to distinguish the different peoples inhabiting that vast land. The Indians, on the other hand, were convinced that (assuming the world *was* real) realness was reserved for them alone and that anything beyond their horizon, other tribes, for example, was just an undifferentiated, viscous magma; it was nevertheless, since they held it to have at least the appearance of existence, open to classification. Although the way those other tribes lived seemed to them laughable and futile, they knew about them down to the last detail. They considered them simulacra lacking any existence of their own and always referred to them in sarcastic or ironic terms. Nevertheless they knew they were grouped into organized tribes, scattered for leagues about them. Their peculiarities were always a source of amusement and the Indians found everything about them equally inept, useless and ridiculous: whether they were nomadic or settled, lived from fishing or agriculture, regularly ate human flesh or abstained completely, walked around naked or clothed, wore jewellery in their lips, neck or nose, lived beneath shelters made from animal skins or in cities built from stone; whether they smoked certain herbs or hoarded gold or precious stones, travelled on foot or in canoes, worshipped plants, places or ancestors; whether they grew shorter the further north the tribe lived or taller the further south, whether they were peace-loving or warlike. The Indians were the centre of the world and those uncertain and amorphous others merely peripheral. The sailors' inability to distinguish amongst them would have been a further source of merriment.

The plain truth was that the sailors knew nothing. The only thing I could tell for certain from my conversations with them was that since the first day our sailors and soldiers had set foot there a tide of death had swept those lands, which many had at first taken for Paradise. I was soon convinced that the Indians must have been completely wiped out. That first encounter with the soldiers must have decimated them, leaving them with little strength to fight subsequent battles. It is hard for me to imagine the scattered or captive survivors anywhere else but on that yellow beach crisscrossed by the rapid comings and goings of naked bodies. That place was also the centre of the world which they carried within them; the visible horizon around it was made up of concentric rings of problematic reality whose existence became less and less likely the further away one went from that central observation point. I had seen how reluctantly they moved away from there when floods drove them up to higher ground; they tried by every means possible to limit the distance between the usual site of the village and the new one they were forced to move to and returned to settle again on that shore the moment the waters began to subside. It was as if they returned not to their own home but to the very hub of life. For them that place was the home of the world. If anything existed, it could not do so outside of that place. In fact, to say that the place was the home of the world is a mistake on my part since for them that place and the world were one and the same thing. Wherever they went, they carried it within them. They themselves were that place. It was there that they were born and died, that they sowed and worked and, when they went out fishing or hunting, it was there that they brought their catch. Their expeditions were like an elastic extension of the place in which they lived; since they carried it within them, it was as if the place itself went wherever they went. At the same time, it was they who gave reality to the other places they visited: by their mere presence they gave physical reality to the uncertain, formless horizon. They were the resistant nucleus of the world, whose soft outer covering, thanks to their excursions, acquired every now and then transient islands of solid life. When they left, that provisional solidity would vanish. And they returned as soon as they could, for the frail belief that their familiar place gave them was easily eroded by the rigours of absence. Outside it they did not feel on safe ground.

Nor did they feel safe within it. Even on their own territory, they suffered the pitiless laws of a harsh climate. It is true that they and the world were one and the same thing, but the single being they constituted was debilitated by a common uncertainty rather than affirmed by their mutual presence. The world of the Indians was the most real there was, but not because it was the only possible world, nor the best of all possible worlds. Even though they took for granted the non-existence of the others, their own existence was in no way irrefutable. In any case for them the main attribute of all things was precariousness. This was not just because of the difficulty of surviving in the world, because of loss and ultimately death, but rather, or perhaps above all, because of the difficulty of gaining access to it. The mere presence of things did not guarantee their existence. A tree, for

example, was not always sufficient proof in itself of its
existence. It was always somewhat lacking in reality It
was present as if by some miracle, which the Indians
scornfully allowed They did so in exchange for some
useful advantage: fruit, wood, shade. But according to
their internal laws they knew that the effective truth of
that exchange was rather problematic. The tree was
there and they were the tree. Without them there was no
tree but without the tree they too were nothing. Each
was so dependent on the other that any trust was
impossible. The Indians could not trust in the existence
of the tree because they knew that the tree depended on
their existence. However, at the same time, since the tree
contributed by its presence to guaranteeing the existence
of the Indians, the latter could not feel entirely sure of
their own existence. They knew that this, derived as it
was from the tree, was indeed problematic since the tree
appeared to acquire its own existence from the fact that
the Indians accorded it one. The problem came not from
a lack of guarantees but rather from an excess. Moreover,
it was impossible to break the vicious circle and see
things from the outside with an impartial eye which
could lay bare the foundations of those beliefs

Their principal problem was the outer world. They
could not, as they might have wished, see themselves
from outside On the other hand, the impression they
made on me, a stranger from the far horizon, was
precisely their externality; to see their shining, compact
bodies crossing the beach amongst the fires lit and
burning as night fell was like a taste of the indestructible.
To the outsider they seemed immune from doubt and
destruction At first they gave me the sense of being the
measure which defined the place of everything between
earth and sky. Once their terrifying festivities were

over, when one saw how quickly and efficiently they grappled with the harsh universe, it seemed only natural to think that world was made for them and that, even in times of confusion, the Indians were never out of harmony with themselves. I would sometimes study them for hours trying to imagine what they were feeling as they moved and worked beneath the blazing sun, bounded by the physical horizon. I would wonder if those confident hands that grasped bone, wood and fish, that moulded the red clay into the shapes of their dreams, were ever invaded, in contact with the burning air, by any doubt. But their gestures were silent and gave nothing away. Like animals, the Indians seemed coterminous with their actions, and those actions could be said to have exhausted their meaning the instant they were performed. For them the clear, precise present of each harsh day with no beginning or end seemed to be the substance through which they physically moved. They gave the enviable impression of being more present in this world than any other thing. Their lack of joy and their moroseness were evidence that thanks to that general feeling of oneness, happiness and pleasure were superfluous to them. I thought they were glad that their material being and their appetites coincided with what the world provided, and believed they could do without joy. Slowly, however, I began to see that the opposite was true, that they felt they had constantly to make real the apparently solid world so that it did not vanish like a thread of smoke into the evening air.

I understood this as I began to penetrate the quagmire of their language, which was unpredictable, contradictory and apparently formless. I would think I had understood a word only to realize a little later that the same word also meant its exact opposite; as soon as I had established those two meanings, others would surface, without it becoming clear to me why the same word should simultaneously mean so many disparate things. *En-gui*, for example, meant men, people, we, I, to eat, here, to look, inside, one, to wake up and many other things. When they said goodbye they employed the formula, *negh*, which also indicated continuity, which is absurd when you consider that when two men say goodbye to each other it means the exchange of phrases has come to an end. *Negh* then means something like 'And then', as when one says 'and then such and such happened'. Once I heard one of the Indians laughing because the members of a neighbouring tribe cried when a child was born and held great celebrations when someone died. I pointed out to him the oddness of them saying *negh* to each other when they said goodbye. He looked at me long and hard, his eyes half-closed in an expression of distrust and scorn, then went off in silence. There is no equivalent in their language for 'to be'. The closest equivalent they have means 'to seem'. They do not use articles either: if they want to say 'there is a tree' or 'a tree is a tree', they say 'it seems tree'. But 'seems' has more of a feeling of untrustworthiness than sameness. It is more a negative than a positive. It implies an objection more than a comparison. It does not refer to a known image but rather tends to erode perception and diminish its force. The word used to designate appearance also means exteriority, a lie, an eclipse, an enemy.

The curved horizon which at first had seemed to me compact and indisputable was in fact exactly what the Indians' language said it was, a box of tricks and an engine of deceit. In that language, both rough and smooth sound the same, they share the same word as do what is present and what is absent, which can be distinguished only by a slight difference in their pronunciation. For the Indians everything seems and nothing is. And the appearance of things is situated above all in the field of non-existence. The open beach, the transparent day, the cool green of the trees in spring, the otters with their smooth, rippling skin, the yellow sand, the golden-scaled fish, the moon, the sun, the air and the stars, the tools they skilfully and patiently fashioned from recalcitrant materials, in short everything that presented itself clearly to the senses was for them formless and had a vague and sticky underside against which the darkness beat.

Under constant threat of annihilation, the Indians floundered in this inclement world. By its wavering presence the external robbed them of reality and, despite its precarious nature, it was more real than they were. They had the disadvantage of doubt which they had no way of verifying from outside. The whole universe was uncertain; themselves, on the other hand, they apprehended as being a little more certain; but the additional uncertainty of not knowing what the universe thought of itself only diminished its authority. All these lucubrations were much more painful than they seem written down because they knew nothing of them, despite living them out every day. They lived them in every action they performed, with each word they uttered, in everything they built and in their dreams. They wanted by every means possible to make the uncertain, changing world endure. For example, for them wasting an arrow was like shedding a piece of reality. They mended everything and were always sweeping and cleaning. When the floods chased them inland, they would return and settle in the same place as soon as the waters subsided a little. The one known world, however precarious, had to be preserved at all costs. If there was any possibility of being or enduring, that was the one place where they could do so and it had to be made to last. Even when it was unrewarding, they constantly worked at making that one known world real. They had no choice: it was, after all, that or nothing.

They tended and protected this world, trying to increase or rather maintain its reality. If storms or fire demolished huts, if water rotted the canoes, if constant use wore out or broke things, it was because the insidious hidden face of the world, all non-existence and blackness (which is the ultimate truth of all things) had broken its natural bounds and was beginning to gnaw away at the visible world. The women were responsible for household tasks and so the men, when not out fishing or hunting, would spend their time mending things. With their usual speed they hurried from one task to another, and on the rare occasions when there was nothing to mend they would make new things which, under the guise of fulfilling a genuine need, gave them, unconvincingly, the illusion of governing the ungovernable. They hardly ever rested. Resting for them meant losing ground to the viscous dark that enveloped them. Towards the end of winter they did seem calmer but that probably had more to do with the fact that the darkness had in some way relented than that they felt more hopeful. The rough fragment of land they inhabited and which seemed to owe its physical existence to their presence had to be kept whole and, if possible, constant. Any change had to be compensated for, every loss replaced. In form and number the whole had to be maintained more or less the same at all times. That was why whenever someone was dying they would be anxiously awaiting the next birth; a misfortune had to be balanced by some good fortune just as, if they had a stroke of good luck, they could not rest easy until the situation had been restored to its original state by some tolerable mishap. An Indian once tried explaining all this to me and what I understood him to say was this: the world is made up of good and evil, of death and birth; there are old and young, men and women, winter and summer, water and earth, sky and trees. All this must *always* exist; if at any time one thing were missing, then everything would crumble. He explained this to me early on in my stay with them and, since a single word can mean so many things in their language, I cannot be sure this was exactly what he said. Indeed everything I think I know about them comes from uncertain signs, blurred memories and hypothetical interpretations, so that in a sense my story, drawn as it is from so many questionable sources, can mean many things, without any one meaning necessarily being the right one If I understood correctly, for the Indians this world is like a precarious building which cannot remain standing if even one stone is missing. Everything must be present at all times and in all its possible states. When the soldiers advanced up the great river with their firearms at the ready, it was not death they brought but the unnameable. The Indians' one scrap of certitude disappeared in the growing dark. Once scattered the Indians would lose their place on the bright side of the world. I do not think many can have escaped, nor do I think they tried to; the few solitary Indians who did survive in the interior would have been left without a world.

However, as they fell they dragged their destroyers down with them. Since the Indians were its only support, the outer world would have disappeared with them and been plunged into non-existence by the destruction of what had first conceived it. What the soldiers who killed them would never manage to understand was that they too were leaving this world together with their victims. You could say that since the destruction of the Indians the whole universe has been left drifting in the void. If this frail universe had need of foundations in order to exist, the Indians, in the midst of all the doubt, were the most certain thing of all. To call them savages is only proof of ignorance; one cannot use the word 'savage' of beings prepared to shoulder such a responsibility. Despite its fragility, the small tenuous light they carried within them, and which they kept alight only with the greatest difficulty, illuminated with its flickering rays the dark, uncertain circle that was the outer world and whose starting point was their own bodies. The immense sky afforded them no protection. On the contrary it relied on them to be able to spread over the naked land its steadfast canopy of jewels.

Every night for years now I have sat staring at the white wall lit by the flickering of a candle and wondered how those Indians, who were possessed, like all men, of an animal-like passivity, could lose themselves in the negation of what seemed at first sight to be irrefutable. Amongst so many strange things: the predictable sun, the countless stars, the trees that resolutely put on the same green splendour each time their season mysteriously comes round, the river that ebbs and flows, the shimmering yellow sand and summer air, the pulsating body which is born, grows old and dies, all the vast distances and the passing days, enigmas which we all in our innocence believe to be familiar, amongst all these presences that seem oblivious to ours, it is understandable that one day, in the face of the inexplicable, we experience the unpleasant feeling that we are just voyagers through a phantasmagoria, a feeling like the one that would sweep over me when on stage, amongst the painted backdrops, in front of a crowd of sleeping shadows, I saw and heard my companions and myself repeating gestures and pronouncing words devoid of truth. But, despite its intensity, that feeling, which we all have sometimes, does not last and does not go deep enough to unsettle our lives. One day, when we least expect it, it suddenly overwhelms us. For a few moments familiar objects are totally alien to us, inert and remote despite their nearness. The commonest word, one we use all the time, begins to sound strange, detaches itself from its meaning and becomes pure noise. Out of curiosity, we say it again, but no amount of repetition brings back the meaning which before had seemed so obvious to us. On the contrary, the more we repeat the word, the stranger and more unfamiliar it sounds. That absence of meaning invades us uninvited, as it infects the things themselves with an air of unreality which gradually diminishes with the heavy somnolence of the passing days, leaving us with only an aftertaste, a vague memory or a suggestion of doubt which casts a slight shadow over our commerce with the world The dazzling flash of light leaves us blinking and, to escape delirium, we prefer to absolve the world of blame and find the causes of this strangeness in ourselves. It is, of course, infinitely preferable to believe that it is oneself and not the world that falters.

The Indians, however, did not have this consolation. The outer world grew less probable as it grew more distant. They were not totally real but nonetheless reality lay in them or nowhere. For all their fragility, everything depended on their wavering support, as unsteady and ephemeral as a candle flame in the wind. That situation was not born of some fleeting feeling but was the principal truth of the world, and it bit deep into their bones and their language, like the indelible scars left by the torturer. They gambled with the continued existence of the world in their every gesture and word, knowing that the slightest error or act of negligence would destroy it all. That was why they were so unrelentingly diligent and anxious: diligent because the whole day and all that filled it depended on them, and anxious because they could never be certain at any one time that what they built would not come crashing to the ground. In their hands lay the precarious fate of all perishable life. It would take only a moment's inattention for it all to collapse, taking them with it.

Every day of my life for more than fifty years I have wondered over and over where such a feeling could have come from. No doubt their belief in the abyss on the edge of the darkness that continually threatened had its roots in some ancient disaster. Men in some sense are born neutral and equal, and it is their actions, the things that happen to them, that differentiate them. Moreover it was not a particular Indian who entered the world with that belief, it was the whole tribe, and over the years I watched the children, as they grew, step quite naturally into that swamp of uncertainty. Day by day their childish gaiety gave way to the brusqueness of their elders: bright and healthy outside, inside they would slowly wither, overwhelmed by an anxiety which held them in its grip until death. In a different way, the same obsession shone in the gaze of both men and women. A common belief made them all equal: without them, the abyss would only yawn wider and general annihilation follow.

It took me a long time to realize that the reason they were burdened with all these cares was that they ate human flesh. One day an Indian explained to me, with indescribable scorn, that the members of other tribes considered it a rare honour to be eaten by their enemies. This was mentioned in the course of a private conversation during which, naturally, he made no reference to the fact that it was he who ate them. It happened one morning in summer when we had seen the other tribe come down the river in their canoes. We were sitting a little way from the village beneath some willows on the shore and the Indian made a face when he realized who they were: apparently they were a people who never settled in any one place, who travelled tirelessly all year, up and down the great river. What is more — the Indian said, lowering his voice and limiting himself to this one remark — they like to be eaten. However much I questioned him, I could not get him to say anything more. He appeared to despise them because their attitude was so utterly inexplicable to him and he considered their predilection both mistaken and perverse. He seemed to see it as immoral, as if in abandoning their body to the appetite of others they were revealing a kind of voluptuousness. However, eating human flesh was clearly not a custom to be proud of either, for they never spoke of it and even seemed to forget about it completely all year until, at more or less the same time, they would begin all over again. They did it against their will, as if it were impossible for them to abstain or as if the recurrent urge was not the appetite of each individual Indian but of that dark something that ruled them. Allowing oneself to be eaten was demeaning not only because of the shameful voluptuousness it revealed but also, indeed above all else, because becoming the object of an experience was to plunge oneself completely into the outer world, to lose one's reality and put oneself on a par with the inert and unformed, to become bound up in the soft dough of appearances. It was an extreme manifestation of the desire not to be. One had only to see the way the Indians handled the dismembered corpses to realize that for them not a trace of humanity remained in those bloodied limbs. The longing they felt as they watched the flesh roasting was not to rediscover the taste of something alien, but to return to an ancient experience beyond memory. If a sense of ill ease grew in them as they chewed it was because that meat must have had for them the taste of stale shadow and oft-repeated errors. Since the external was pure appearance, they knew deep down that they were chewing on nothing. Yet they were obliged to repeat that empty gesture again and again in order to continue to enjoy at all costs that exclusive and precarious existence that allowed them the illusion of being, on the barren crust of that desolate land traversed by wild rivers, the only true men.

Over the years, the evidence slowly mounted up: each summer, the Indians' swift and diligent hands pushed out their canoes in readiness to leave for some previously agreed destination, driven by a desire whose origins lay in some far distant time and place. They knew no other way of separating themselves from the world, no other way of becoming, in their own eyes, a little more defined, more whole, less enmeshed in the dull improbability of things. For a time, until once more it lost its power, they drew from the meat they devoured and the bones they chewed and sucked at with such terrible perseverance their own frail and transient sense of being. They acted in this way because at some time, before they understood their individual identity in the world, they had experienced the reality of the void. That must have happened before they began eating the flesh of those who were not true men, those from outside. Before, in the dark years when they floundered with the others, they used to eat each other. Only now, as I too near the void, am I beginning to understand: the Indians only began to feel they were true men when they stopped eating each other. Finding an alternative to that mutual predatoriness changed them. They turned towards the outside world and became the tribe that formed the centre of the world, ringed by a horizon whose outer limits became more problematic the further it was from that centre. Despite the fact that they too were from that unlikely world, they struggled up to a new level of existence. Thus, even while their feet were still sunk deep in the primeval mud, their heads, liberated, inhaled the clean air of truth.

However, from their obvious anxiety it was clear that their victory was by no means irreversible. It was as if the old danger was still there. Whatever ground they had gained could always be lost. They knew that they were the most substantial beings in this world but they could never be sure that they were real enough, never believe that they had reached an unassailable level of reality that would not crumble. Above all, their old, confused, rudimentary sense of nothingness which they brought with them from the past became their way of being. If it is true, as some people say, that we always try to repeat our early experiences and in some way succeed in so doing, the anxiety the Indians felt must have had its origins deep in the past, in the bitter aftertaste their desire still left them with even though the object of that desire had changed. They could not get any true grasp on reality because they knew deep in their hearts that,

whatever object of desire they chose, however unreal
and lacking in individuality the people they ate seemed to
them, the only point of reference they had by which to
recognize the taste of that alien flesh was the memory of
their own. The Indians knew, as surely as night follows
day, that the force that drove them out towards the far
horizon in search of human flesh was not the desire to
devour the inexistent but the more ancient, more deep-
rooted desire to eat one another. They were thus the
cause and the object of that anxiety. They knew themselves without knowing it and they carried out acts
whose meaning, they knew, was not what it appeared to
be. The true aim of those acts was rather the pursuit of
what was apparently the least likely and furthest removed object of their desire: themselves. Although
doubtless they never clearly acknowledged it, they knew
the real purpose behind their expeditions. In their quest
for the taste they had once known, they took an
immensely circuitous detour to the outside world. For a
while this simulacrum satisfied them. They allowed
themselves to fall, drunk and blind, into the blackness in
order to emerge slowly into a brighter, more orderly day
which, with the passing of another year, would in turn
degenerate. They did not want to think about those
events because they had experienced them from the
inside and had no illusions about what really lay behind
them. Somewhat incredulous at the persistence of that
recurring hunger which each time they thought to have
sated once and for all, they resorted, as a tribe, to
concocting an elaborate explanation which set out as
plain as day the irrefutable proof of their existence and
their innocence. But, however convincing the proofs
they came up with, they could not erase something they
carried with them from the start. They only half-

deceived themselves. They had been party to a blind pact in which they, the underdogs, always came off worst. For them the world could not be of much value because they knew that in their essential actions even the only true men, those who seemed to have hauled themselves up out of the dark, still trailed the dark, sticky dough of formlessness, into whose swamp no steady, continuous light could penetrate.

In that uncertain world there was an exact place for each man and each object. In the work carried out communally each Indian performed his task at just the right moment, but I could not have told you who had given the order or when it had been given. When they went out in the canoes each man had his own place: the ones who took up the paddles did so as if it had been decided beforehand that it was their turn to row. It was the same when they went out hunting or fishing, or when they went to war. The women, who sowed, reaped and did the household chores, behaved in exactly the same way. Never erring, never taking someone else's place, they filled the role required of them at a particular moment without, it seemed, external guidance. I never saw anyone perform what could be called a random act. Every action, however insignificant, was part of a pre-established order. I slowly realized that some actions that had seemed absurd at first were, in fact, of vital importance. Beneath an indifferent sky, within the ambit of the two or three leagues of land they inhabited, each human action was aimed at preserving the dubious stability of a world under the continual threat of destruction. Even the mildest, most limpid of days was contaminated by that threat. Each movement shored up a world on the point of collapse; each act was like a form imposed on things to keep them from disintegrating;

each watchful, worried look simply sought reassurance that the flimsy order of their world had deigned to continue, at least for a few moments more. Like every visible thing in this gleaming, empty space, I too had my place in the overall strategy.

The role I was given enabled me to survive. Each time they went off in search of human beings for their annual festivals, the Indians brought back with them one person like me whom they did not kill and who was treated for a while to a life of luxurious ease before being sent back. For ten years I watched a succession of these contemptuous guests come and go. The Indians would keep them for two or three months, sometimes less, and, once the orgy was over and the tribe had reverted to its calm, monotonous way of life, they would let them go. They only kept me with them for so many years because they did not know where I should be returned to; the minute they saw men who looked like me, they put me in a canoe and sent me off downriver. Of all their guests I was the only one who did not know how to behave; it was as if the others knew what the Indians expected of them and this knowledge gave them the right to seem distant and arrogant. They already knew before they arrived what it took me years to grasp. When they first landed on that yellow coast and were addressed by the Indians with a gently insistent *Def-ghi, def-ghi*, they knew exactly what it meant. For me, on the other hand, puzzling that out was like fighting my way through dense, intractable jungle. And since the Indians considered the world around them to be dependent on them, they never imagined that I might not understand their language or intentions. In fact, for them I had no existence of my own and, accordingly, I could not fail to understand what they expected of me. Not once did they offer an explanation. I realize now that even the first looks they gave me that first night as I walked amongst the fires expressed not just a desire to attract my attention and to ingratiate themselves, but also the somewhat lewd insistence of one party reminding another party of the conditions of a secret pact. It was years before I could sift out some meaning from their opaque language and glimpse (for I could never be sure I was right) the exact meaning of those two shrill, swift syllables which they used to designate my person. Like all the other syllables that made up the Indians' language those two sounds, *def-ghi*, had many disparate and contradictory meanings. *Def-ghi* was what they called people absent or asleep, or people who were tactless, or visitors who outstayed their welcome; and *def-ghi* was the name they gave to a bird with a black beak and green and yellow plumage that they would sometimes tame and which made them laugh because it repeated certain words they taught it, as if it really had the gift of speech. *Def-ghi* was also the name given to certain objects the Indians put in the place of someone absent and which they used to represent the person at meetings, even setting food before them as if expecting them to eat in place of the man represented. *Def-ghi* was what they used for things reflected in water; something that lasted a long time was *def-ghi*; I had noticed too, shortly after my arrival, that when children played they applied *def-ghi* to any child who took up a position outside the circle and started pulling faces and mimicking some character. And *def-ghi* was a man who went on ahead of an expedition and came back to report what he had seen, or a man who went to spy on the enemy and brought back details of their movements, or a man who in certain meetings would sometimes start to make a speech out loud but as if talking to himself. All

these things and many others were *def-ghi*. After long
reflection I decided that the reason they had given me
that name was because they wanted me to share some
common essence with everything else that was *def-ghi*.
They wanted me to reflect like water the image they
gave of themselves, to repeat their gestures and words,
to represent them in their absence, and, when they
returned me to my fellow creatures, they wanted me to
be like the spy or scout who witnesses something that
the rest of the tribe has not yet seen and retraces his
steps and recounts it, meticulously. Threatened by
everything that controls us from the dark and keeps us
outside in the open until the day we are plunged by one
sudden capricious gesture back into the indistinct, the
Indians wanted there to be a witness to and a survivor of
their passage through this material mirage; they wanted
someone to tell their story to the world.

The most arduous and dangerous moments in that
difficult existence occurred when they abandoned themselves to their overwhelming desire and risked stepping
out like sleepwalkers into deepest night. They had the
sense to keep the cooks apart from all that to look after
them like gentle shepherds (albeit of wolves, not sheep).
And then, as their final card, they had their disdainful
guest fully aware of how dependent they were on his
mood and his memory and his willingness to carry with
him into an unbelieving world, which had clothed them
in such a threadbare reality, some strong, entire and
immediately recognizable image of them. Thus they
would be allowed to live on in the visible world after their
fleeting selves had long since vanished without trace.
Another reason they always ensured that such guests
were present on the days they partook of human flesh
was to demonstrate beyond doubt how valiantly they

had dragged themselves up and out from the primeval slime. They wanted to prove to the vast, formless world that, because they had learned to distinguish between the internal and external worlds, between what now stood in the luminous air and what was still floundering in the dark, they had become the sole support of that harsh reality, the one true people. During those cruel days, they needed us as witnesses to their innocence. Should they succumb to the void, we were to carry to the alien horizon proof of their existence. Scattered throughout the world, we were the last glowing embers of the fire that consumed them. They released us so that we might carry the news of that annihilation. In the silent night the smell of whitewashed walls and honeysuckle wafts through the open window and, while I have strength to write, the point of my quill scratches its way slowly across the rough surface of the paper, leaving nothing more than an echo of that murmur that speaks to me from who knows where across years of silence and disdain.

That is how, sixty years later, the Indians still dwell, unvanquished, in my memory. I cannot think of them without seeing, too, the immense, blue, luminous sky that filled with stars each night. When there was no moon there was an infinite number of those enormous, sparkling stars. In winter they shone in icy hues of scintillating greens, blues, violets, reds and yellows. Now I realize that they were only there — encircling us, that sliver-thin fringe of palpitating fear and ignorance — because at every moment, without respite, the Indians held them there. The great river that reflected them and was filled in turn with gleaming lights flowed towards the south with the breath they breathed into it, and the trees grew green again each spring because the blood of the Indians mingled with the sap. Each day they paid what they could of the unpayable price demanded of them for having half hauled themselves out of the swamp which gave them life and which left them with an unending sense of disorientation. Many of the memories which track like meteors across my mind during the day are of the land near the wide river whose surface was furrowed by the canoes that sped across it in all directions. And many of the purely mechanical gestures I make, often at the most unexpected moments, seem impregnated with those memories, at times in such obscure and secret ways that even I fail to see there is a connection. Yet I still have the strange feeling that in performing just such a fleeting, insignificant action, all the years I spent there will suddenly rise to the surface from the dark region in which they lie buried. To these memories, which my conscious mind contemplates day after day like so many painted images, are added those other memories which only the body recalls; they reappear without ever actually having been registered by the memory in order to be carefully retained and subjected to the scrutiny of reason. Those memories do not present themselves as images but rather in the form of tremors, bodily cramps, palpitations, inaudible murmurings and tremblings. Going out into the clear morning air one's body recalls, without recourse to memory, a similar air which enveloped it in just the same way in years long past. I can honestly say that, in its own way, my whole body remembers those years of intense, carnal life which seem to have penetrated it so deeply that it has grown insensible to any other experience. Just as the Indians from some of the neighbouring tribes used to trace an invisible circle in the air to protect themselves from the unknown, my body, wrapped in the skin of those years, now lets nothing in from the outside. Only what resembles it is acceptable. The present moment is only of interest insofar as it bears some relation to the past. The Indians were quite right about me; the confused glitter of that past is the only story I have to tell. Moreover, since I owe them my life, it is only fair that I should repay them by each day reliving their lives.

But it is not easy. These assiduous memories cannot always be grasped; at times they seem clear, austere, precise, all of a piece; but as soon as I make a move to take hold of them and fix them, they start to unfold and expand, and details which, seen from a distance, had been obscured by the whole, then multiply, proliferate and take on an importance they hitherto lacked. There comes a point when I grow dizzy and find it difficult to establish a hierarchy amongst all these presences competing for my attention. I no longer know what is the centre of the memory and what is the periphery: the centre of each memory seems to scatter in all directions and, as each detail of the whole continues to grow, other forgotten details appear, multiplying and increasing in their turn. Often I begin to feel disconsolate and I tell myself then that not only is the world infinite but also every one of its parts, and therefore my memories too. On days like that I know enough to say that the Indians, in keeping me so long with them, could not hope to protect me from the evil that gnawed at them. At other times, however, many of these images appear with great calm in close, clear ranks and are more enduring. They come and go thanks to a mysterious and constant force which not only lets them preserve their individual distinguishing features but also seems to smooth and polish them until they are firm and clean as pebbles or bones.

Curiously enough, one of these memories is of the
children I saw the day after my arrival playing far from
the huts, on the shore I often saw them happily playing
the same game beneath the quiet sun. In my ten years
there the group changed, for when the boys reached a
certain age they would be taken off for a few days to one
of the islands accompanied by some of the hunters; when
they returned, looking rather sterner than when they
left, they were men. But since the group was made up of
children of all ages, the smaller ones created a kind of
continuity, so that it always seemed to me to be the same
group I had seen on that first day. In the beginning, it
was very difficult for me to distinguish individuals since
they all looked so alike with their straight, jet-black hair
and dark, glossy bodies and I did not notice the changes
and thought they always were the same children. And it
is true that they did try to keep everything the same at all
times and thus create an illusion of immobility. I must
have seen those children playing hundreds of times but
in my mind it is always the same memory, the scene on
the first day, which returns more clearly and more
persistently each time. I had escaped to the beach in
order not to see the horrific butchery that was taking
place under the blazing sun. The lazy play of the children
calmed me and I stayed there for a long time, watching
them. They stood in a line, parallel to the river, with just
a small space between each of them, then fell, one by one,
and lay on the ground as if asleep. When the last one in
the line had fallen, the first came and stood behind him,
all the others followed and the game started again.
Sometimes the last child would rest his hands on those of
the child in front, and that child on the hands of the next
and so on up to the first in the line. Then, linked in this
way, they would move forwards in a straight line or form

a circle, or coil round to make a spiral. For hours the children would happily play this game, the bright, enduring memory of which visits me constantly. I do not know why but I imagine I can see in this memory, which grows clearer with the years, some obscure sign from the world surfacing to the light of day. Perhaps it is because I find it hard to accept that the game's persistence through many generations of children and its insistent presence in my memory should be mere chance and have no significance whatsoever when measured against infinity. Such determination to endure in the unfriendly light of the world suggests, perhaps, some complicity with its deepest essence. Like the form time takes or the reason for the existence of space, this game partakes of the structure of the elemental, which reproduces the ebbs and flows of human blood with its rushes, its discoveries, its palpitations. But even if no hidden meaning were revealed, every time that game reappears in my memory it is in an ever simpler form. All the extraneous, contingent details are pared away to leave the clean, geometric lines of the figures that the children formed with their bodies on the sand: a discontinuous line created when the children fragmented the straight line by falling down to lie in pretended sleep, only to re-form later by resting their hands on the shoulders of the child in front to make a chain which would then be transformed into a circle or a spiral.

Another memory which frequently visits me, always in accordance with its own mysterious rhythm, is of one summer dawn, the day after one of the festivals. An Indian lay dying on the sand. He was on his back with his face to the pale air. His body was a mass of wounds, bruises and burns. He had spent the previous day eating human flesh, getting drunk and copulating. His wide eyes were staring up at the livid sky and a trail of blood and saliva trickled out from the corner of his half-open mouth and dried in the cool morning air. As the man approached death, the summer sun rose in the sky which grew bluer once the initial paleness of dawn was past. The contrast offered by the dying man and the place in which his life was ebbing away seemed proof that the world robs us of our very substance and feeds upon our blood. For, as the light in his eyes went out and his breathing became weaker and more laboured, the morning sun grew in brilliance and magnificence, just as if the world were taking from the man's last breath the gleams of light which darted over the water, intensifying the yellow of the sand and the blue of the sky, and which were reflected by the sharp green leaves on the trees. The man was only a little older than me. As I remained crouched by his side, he was no longer aware of my presence. To the extent that I could know any of the Indians, I knew the man fairly well; he lived with his family in a hut very close to mine and often sent the women or children across with food or brought it himself. I had been very struck by his discretion and dignity. Although for weeks or even months the Indians would forget my presence or accept it with indifference, most of the time they besieged me with their exaggerated poses, their demands and their flattery. It was not uncommon, for example, for them to make a great fuss whenever they brought me food, no doubt to ensure that when I spoke of them on some hypothetical future occasion I would mention their generosity. They emphasized all their actions and characteristics in order to make themselves more accessible and more easily comprehensible The poses they adopted did not always reveal them in the best of lights; however, they did not much mind whether the image they gave of themselves was good or bad; what was important was that it should be intense and memorable. Many of them pursued me for the ten years I was there with puerile details which they would act out each time we met. On the very first day, one Indian, trying to attract my attention, made as if to eat me and pretended to chew on his own arm. Every time he saw me he would remind me of this and laugh. *Def-ghi, def-ghi*, he would say, adding a few more rapid sounds which could roughly be translated as: I'm the one who made the joke about eating you. He aged in those ten years and lost almost all his teeth; he was a squat, broad-built man whose smile revealed pale pink gums and crinkled the skin round his eyes. Never, in all the time I was with them, did that Indian say anything else to me: just the same two or three shrill, rapid noises to fix in my memory that childish joke which, because it was unforgettable, would save him. Sometimes he would pass by me looking very serious and distracted and continue on his way without a greeting. Then, as if suddenly remembering, he would call after me, give me his artificial smile, utter the formulaic words and then, serious again, walk off. The afternoon they sent me off downriver in the canoe, I spotted him for the last time, pushing his way through the crowd pressing round the canoe, trying hard to keep smiling amidst all the shoving, and endlessly repeating the sounds which the noise of the crowd prevented me from hearing but which I could easily guess: *Def-ghi, def-ghi, I'm the one who made the joke about eating you. I'm the one who made the joke about eating you.*

Although not everyone went to such extremes, virtually all the Indians behaved in the same way. Those fixed, unsubtle poses with which they would try to catch my attention, whenever opportunity allowed, were their attempt to escape the anonymous void When they claimed good qualities for themselves, they were immeasurably vain. One made out he was the best huntsman of the tribe, another that he made the best arrows, another that he bathed himself more often than anyone else They were not in the habit of lying but on some occasions I noticed that they would exaggerate, not in order to deceive me, but to increase in their own eyes, and in mine too, the solidity of the character they represented. One morning an old man boasted to me how all his teeth had fallen out at once; a woman used all kinds of circumlocutions, unusual in the Indians, to cover up the fact she might be exaggerating, and told me that when she was still a virgin everyone wanted her to be the one to chew the roots they made their alcoholic brew from because her saliva was so sweet. She spat on the tips of her fingers and held them out to me, saying that it was a taste I would never again forget. This desire to make a strong, lasting impression was not the only obstacle to forming friendships or at least a simple, natural relationship with them. Their stiffness, which sometimes bordered on a brusque sullenness, made it impossible to get close to them. The shared happiness, genuine and liberating, that at one time or another everyone feels, was unknown to them. They seemed to have forbidden themselves all elemental pleasures. They withered under the rigorous, self-imposed obligation to appear sad or serious. They forced themselves into a narrow, arid life from which, wary, they banished pleasure. The effect of that moroseness was especially evident when they did experience spontaneous pleasure. It would attack them despite their constant rejection of it, provoking in them a desperate inner battle which threw up many contradictory emotions What they disliked most about pleasure was feeling it. As long as it remained absent from their lives the decision to banish it seemed perfectly feasible. When it did appear, in the form of sensual pleasure or just simple happiness at some unexpected event, they tried to hide it and appeared embarrassed or ashamed. They did not want to recognize their own pleasure. They did not like it when something broke through their defences enough to please them.

The man who was slowly dying as he lay face up on the yellow sand that morning was different. The anxiety and rigidity of the Indians was less marked in him. More than any of the others he seemed prepared to let himself go and allow himself to be shaped by the ebb and flow of the days, without struggling either to forge a particular image of himself or negate the rhythms of chance. That flexibility allowed me to have a rather more direct and natural relationship with him. We did not become intimate friends and we rarely exchanged more than a few words but I knew that when we met he would not give me one of those inevitable obsequious smiles or try to leave me with some ineradicable impression He even walked a little more slowly than the others. Without quite realizing it I recognized in that almost imperceptible indolence a kind of originality. It was as if he personally believed that the negation of all other possibilities which was an essential aspect of all things, of their language, of the flesh of his people, was perhaps not so absolute after all. Even if it was, in spite of everything and though annihilation awaited him, he reserved for himself the freedom to defy the rigid laws of the world and to live a life different from that of the others. A sort of kindness emanated from that minute difference. I often visited him and he came to my house quite frequently Generally we spoke very little but I felt that his mere presence was evidence of a certain compassion. He taught me how to fish with spears and arrows and with those small bone knives which the Indians were so skilled at making and using. He was patient and affectionate with children. When the men were discussing something they would often ask his opinion and he would give it clearly and unemphatically, with a thoughtful air which seemed to show that he judged his own words to be less infallible than his respectful companions. It was as if, secretly believing them incapable of withstanding more oppressive truths, he were, in a fatherly way, confirming the others' false hopes.

The year before he had been one of the cooks but in previous years I had not known him well enough to distinguish him from other members of the tribe. Confusing their temporary function with a more permanent state, I had been led by the serene, vigilant attitude of the cooks to think that they always behaved like that. I could not grasp the reasoning behind the appointment of the cooks although I knew that, according to a system of ethics I did not understand, the hunters of the prisoners had to abstain from eating their flesh. The hunters were chosen each year only after long, confidential discussions. The first time I noticed this man, he was preparing a frugal meal for the cooks, far from the tumult of the rest of the tribe, and I associate him in my memory with the calm, precise gestures of that moment. But that image of him clouded other facts: for example, the fact that the day before the same man had murdered those whom the tribe was now devouring and had doubtless spent the morning using his little bone knife to chop up the bodies of the captives as they lay on a carpet of green leaves However, during the following year my image of him as a man of calm precision was confirmed by the warm good sense he showed in all he did

His death showed me how wrong I was. The day before should have prepared me for disillusionment. In the morning I had seen how anxiously he watched the cooks as skilfully and impassively they arranged the butchered bodies over the glowing embers. His expression was unequivocal, showing no trace of any inner struggle or doubt. He prowled around the smoking grills even more impatiently than the others. In many of the Indians a slow, dreamy, distracted half-smile betrayed their anticipation of the real pleasure soon to come. His face showed not a hint of this spurious joy: sullen, withdrawn, almost furious, he paced back and forth near the grills, clearly oblivious to any other sounds the world might offer. I began to observe him from a distance, trying not to lose sight of him. When the meat was ready, I was horrified to see him punch a woman on the shoulder to make her move out of the way. He picked up his piece of meat with the same air of sullen withdrawal he had shown while waiting and then, like a distracted animal, looked about for a quiet place to sit and eat it. He walked alone to the river's edge and sat down in an empty canoe to eat. He chewed stubbornly and with growing frenzy, barely raising his head from the meat, as if silently furious that he was not able with one bite to devour not just his piece of meat but the whole world that contained it. When he had finished the first piece he jumped up from the canoe and went determinedly to fetch another. He took it and remained by the fire to eat it, finished it in two bites, then asked for a third helping. He was obviously already full but that third piece seemed like a deliberate duty he had imposed on himself With the meat in his hand he began to walk slowly along the shore, almost keeping time with his chewing, pausing now and then with his mouth open. He could not bring himself to swallow the last few mouthfuls. Frowning and staring into the distance, he kept on chewing what remained of the forgotten piece of meat that he still grasped in the hand that swung at his side as he walked. He finished it with difficulty. When the bone was clean of meat, he distractedly let it fall onto the sand in which his feet had left deep tracks. Then he dropped to the ground. For a while he dozed in the sun until the noise of the other Indians milling round the jars of alcohol roused him and made him half sit up and stare blinking in their direction. The next day he would lie dying on that same beach, but in that precise moment he seemed completely cut off from the world which had apparently lost all physical reality for him Still heavy with sleep he got up and walked over to the jars. He did not even notice that one of the Indians distributing the alcohol was holding a full bowl out to him; instead he picked up one from the ground, plunged it into the container, filled it and emptied it in one draught. He repeated this six or seven times, standing rigid and erect, his chest a little puffed out, his eyes growing ever more clouded, revealing that behind their opacity lay not tumultuous dreams but merely a thick, endless blackness Then he moved away from the crowd and until nightfall stood stiff and motionless near the water's edge. It took an immense effort to keep up that rigid immobility and it was obvious that his whole body was struggling to maintain it. His neck swelled up and heavy, twisting veins stood out on his forehead; his eyes were fixed and staring, his teeth so tightly clenched that drops of saliva oozed from between them His immobility seemed all the stranger in contrast to the febrile activity around him in which the whole tribe was engaged. For some time now bodies, in pairs or groups, mingling Indians of all ages, from children to old men and women, had been locked in brute embraces, filling the smooth, warm night air with their sighs, shouts and laments. Many were rolling around on the sand only yards from his tense, erect figure. Then suddenly, completely unexpectedly, just as night closed in, he ran off and disappeared into the trees and the dark. I lost sight of him. I know he joined in the frenzy, plunging again and again into the swamp that opened up for a few hours each year, swallowing the tribe whole, returning a few of them badly battered and keeping others for ever. The hours of immobility he had subjected himself to had in no way been a display of control or a superhuman attempt to protect himself from the chaos; on the contrary, it had been a gesture of wild defiance, yet another form of delirium and excess. In any event, in the livid dawn which followed that endless night, the darkness washed up on the yellow beach only the bruised and empty shell of the man I had known.

Bent over him in the morning sun, I watched him dying. Unlike the other memory, which is made up of many different experiences which have fused to form a single image in my memory, this one is unique because the death of every man is unique and it was that man and no other who was dying. In this respect death and memory are identical: they are unique to each man, and men who think that because they have shared similar experiences with others they therefore share common memories fail to realize that everyone's memories are different and that they are condemned to the solitude of those memories as surely as they are to the solitude of their own death. Those memories are a prison for each man in which he remains confined from birth to death.

They are his death. It is because of their uniqueness that each man dies, because that is what dies, that is what is transient and never reborn in others, that is what amongst the crowds is doomed to die: the unique memories which feed the illusion of a shared rememberer whom death will ultimately erase. And that morning I learned from the battered man, now scarcely breathing, that virtue cannot save us from the surrounding blackness. Even if we have the courage to find our way through one night, a little way off another longer night awaits us. In vain he had, in calmer days, striven to be good; the gaping mouth over which he danced, innocent and poised, devoured him anyway. Our lives are lived in a place of terrible indifference which recognizes neither virtue nor vice and annihilates us all without compunction, without apportioning good or evil. At midday the man at last stopped breathing. Amidst blue sky, green leaves, golden river and yellow sand, he became just a blurred, nameless blotch, as if the extravagant outward show of the world about us had plundered him of his breath and his very substance and rendered it up to the light.

However vivid a dream may have been and however clear it remains in the memory, no sooner has the dream passed than it becomes unreal and remote for the dreamer. If he tells it to someone else, the person listening to him only fools himself into believing that he recognizes the details and grasps its meaning. These are problematic even for the dreamer. If one afternoon, for example, a forgotten dream returns to him, prompted by something that has happened in his waking hours, there is no way he can verify the exact moment he had that dream and he will be unable to determine if he dreamt it last night, or a month ago or even many years before. He will have no way of knowing if that dream, which he thought he had forgotten, really is an old dream remembered or a brand new one which suddenly appears to him for the first time in the guise of a memory. Memories and dreams are made of the same stuff. And you will see on reflection that everything is memory. However, the world can place them in time and lend them substance. If at this moment, for example, I were to remember a dream in which Father Quesada appeared, his presence in it would date the dream, since I could not have dreamed it before I met him, and the memory of Father Quesada, which allows him an existence independent of my dreams, takes on substance and reality thanks to a few books he gave me before he died and which I always keep with me. In that way, dream, memory and harsh experience are defined and intertwined to form the piece of loosely woven fabric I rather unenthusiastically call my life. But sometimes in the silence of the night, my hand stops its writing and in the clear, almost ungraspable present, I find it hard to know if that life full of different continents, seas, planets and human hordes really did take place or if it was just the vision of a moment provoked more by my drowsiness than by any exalted frame of mind. The Indians' use of 'seem' for 'be' was not after all such a wild distortion. Quite often I have had to give due deference to the truth of some of their beliefs.

One day, for example, when dusk was falling, I was sitting quietly at the door of my hut, my mind pleasantly vacant. It had been one of those long spring days buffeted by a warm, gentle wind that had blown until dusk, chasing thick, white clouds behind which one glimpsed snatches of brilliant blue. By then it was a spent force but had left the sky clear of clouds apart from two

or three long, almost transparent strands that lay
superimposed one on top of the other and formed
twisting, parallel paths that the sun's rays tinged green
and orange. Sitting on the newly swept floor, my back
against the adobe wall, I watched them slowly disappear
from the smooth, darkening sky. The wind seemed to
have blown my mind clear of thoughts just as it had
cleared the sky of clouds I watched the remaining cloud
fragments changing from violet to blue as they thinned
and finally vanished. The sun had already sunk below the
horizon and the light that lit the evening came from its
last dying rays.

The dusk calmed the village. Like me, some of the
Indians were resting in the entrances to their huts. A
little way off others, more indolent than usual (or at least
so they seem to me now in my memory), were strolling
up and down the beach. One man was kneeling down to
light a fire Several children, obscured by the penumbra
of the trees, were absorbed in their strange games.
Perhaps it was because the restless wind had died down
that the evening, the people and the curved horizon
heavy with mystery seemed more constant and benevolent. A smell of cooking drifted on the air without
tainting its freshness. For a few minutes I amused myself
by observing the dark people wandering around me as if
bewitched and when I looked up again the last small
clouds had gone. The empty sky was a smooth blue that
grew slowly darker and the first stars began to appear, as
if approaching from afar, so faint at first you had to look
hard to see them They were just tiny tenuous points of
light that seemed to flare up and die down, flare up and
die down, as if the effort of existing cost them, that many
consider eternal, the same in blood, sweat and tears as it
does us

At that time I believed that my fate was set and that my brief, monotonous future would end in death. I did not know then that only a short time afterwards the Indians would send me off in a canoe loaded with goods on my way to a summer night, so distant and so different from the days I took to be my final lot. But there was no frenzy or anxiety in that belief of mine. I just abandoned myself indifferently to my fate and gave myself over to what the present might bring Having come naked into this world, my daily bread, however dry, sufficed and I knew of no better tastes that might justify feelings of nostalgia. In that peaceful night I felt even emptier than usual but, perhaps because of the clement weather, was unaware of it. I remained seated for a few moments watching the stars come out and then got up and began to walk through the village.

A few Indians gave me the knowing, conspiratorial looks which, after so many years, I had grown accustomed to. *Def-ghi, def-ghi*, they said, pointing to themselves as they passed, half-closing their eyes or making some grimace. Others, indifferent, did not even notice me. Sometimes the noise of splashing came from the nearby river. The man who had been trying to light a fire a few minutes before, had succeeded. As he mixed dry straw and twigs from bushes with the firewood, tall, vertical flames leaped up, spluttering and crackling furiously. Almost simultaneously, from out of the blue penumbra, a host of dark butterflies flew into the flames. Near the fire the warm air grew hot and, although no wind was blowing, such was the violence with which the fire had taken hold that it began to send up turbulent clouds of smoke. The man poked at the firewood with a stick, removing the smaller branches scattered on the ground. Some passing Indians shouted brief greetings to him

then went off into the blue shadows. I left behind me the
tumult of smoke, sparks and flames and walked towards
the river. In the blue darkness, the sand glittered more
yellow than in the light of day. A man came out of the
river and disappeared into the trees. I stopped by the
shore.

The shadow there remained steady, but no denser. I
thought it odd not to hear the birds which usually sang
so loudly at dusk. In fact they had been silent for some
time. Apart from the waves almost imperceptibly lapping
the shore at regular intervals, even the water was still.
There were only insistent human noises and voices:
shouts, greetings, conversations, the noise of bone and
wood being used by the Indians to make recognizable
shapes out of the formlessness. Behind me I occasionally
heard the dull thud of bare feet coming and going,
running and sliding over the sand. A little further off,
several boats were silhouetted on the shore where it was
darker still. Everything present, including ourselves,
was in the place and, at the same time, was the place.
Indeed, we, even more than the place itself, were that
place, and, because it seemed more welcoming that
night, there was something wounding about its usual
scornful silence. The peace laid the evening bare. The
fact that we only endured because it let us, placed us on a
level lower even than the submissive and impassive
beasts. According to the Indians, it was thanks to our
seeming to be that the place seemed a place at all and yet
it did nothing, made neither sign nor attempt to win our
trust.

The firm sand on the shore made my bare feet wet. In
my distracted frame of mind it took me a few seconds to
notice that, for some time now, the sand had been
glittering white and phosphorescent. I saw that the river

was the same colour. I raised my head and, turning round, looked up at the sky: it was the moon. I had never seen it so large, round and brilliant. It shone so brightly that it erased all stars from the sky. It rose slowly, irrefutable and unique, warm and familiar, and the intensity of its light explained why, at a certain moment, the darkness had ceased to spread. Now everything that was visible was adorned with spots of moonlight that spilled onto the leaves of the trees; it printed patches of pure white on the ground, on the walls and roofs of the houses, on the naked bodies which, as they moved amongst the trees, gleamed with a cold, constant fire. It had the friendly proximity of those things we do not understand but which no longer frighten us because, who knows why, we have accepted their mystery. Nothing justified its presence and yet, seeing it so often, closer and gentler than the blinding sun, with its phases, its comings and goings, constant and regular enough to be predictable, in many ways helping us order our lives, it calmed rather than disquieted us. Every day the scornful sun passed over to shed its crude light on the unjustified persistence of this place which was also us, while the gentle moon, by its very nearness, formed part of that place and built a sort of bridge between the remote and the familiar Because of the moon everything that drifted unfinished in the darkness seemed at least to acknowledge us and promise a less arbitrary annihilation. Although it was incapable of saving us or interceding on our behalf, the moon, a warm and constant companion, could give us the illusion that we were being measured from outside by criteria not so very different from those we applied ourselves

Generally the Indians went to bed early but on those warm nights many lingered outside their huts until it was completely dark. The Indian who had lit the fire had done so for no other reason than to pass the time stirring the embers and feeding them with wood that he gathered from nearby. As he leaned in to poke at the wood with his stick, the growing flames made his dark body gleam. Absorbed in his work, he seemed oblivious to the moon mounting in the sky behind him, its unusual size and astonishing, perfect roundness, its strange blue-white brilliance, its presence, obvious and urgent. The light it gave out, neither nocturnal nor diurnal, seemed to hint at some imminent event. It grew more and more intense and the bright white patches slipping through the foliage and reflected in the river began to fade and be absorbed into the general brilliance. Even the flames of the fire paled in that tempered luminosity The light, which until a few moments before had been scattered and arbitrary, had become a uniform clarity bestowing an added strangeness on objects whose reality was already dubious. I had a sudden confused feeling that perhaps we were not where we thought we were or who we thought we were and that by its rare brightness the strange light was about to reveal our true condition to us.

Almost at the same moment as it reached maximum intensity, showering everything below with light, it began to mask itself. I noticed it at the same time as some Indians who were strolling between the village and the beach. None of them had been watching the moon, but for some inexplicable reason they all felt it at the same time as I, who had not taken my eyes off it for a good while. A slowly advancing blueness was superimposing itself on and gradually diminishing the astonishing brilliance. The unmasked part seemed even brighter in contrast, but that too was being overtaken by the blue penumbra. A clear vertical line was dividing the moon into two parts; the blue part continued its slow growth, like a bow stretched wider and wider as the brilliant part grew narrower. A few minutes later the vertical line had divided the moon in two halves: one blue, the other still intensely bright. If you looked closely, however, on the outer edge of the blue half you could see a new vertical line beginning to encroach on the other half and creep imperceptibly towards the centre. The bright half was shrinking and in just a few moments would be gone.

The man who had been playing with the fire dropped the stick he had been using to stir the embers, looked up at the moon and trudged down to the middle of the beach. When he left the fire, his body, which had shone in the glow of the flames, lost its clarity and became a bluish silhouette slightly more solid than the penumbra through which it moved. He walked on with some difficulty and disappeared amongst the other Indians who were silently leaving their houses, appearing from amongst the trees or from the part of the village that extended inland, to gather on the open space of the beach. You could hear the sound of feet on sand, of many people breathing, of hands carelessly brushing their own or other people's bodies, but not one voice rose from the growing throng staring at the sky. Despite the silence a breath of certainty floated in the thickening dark With my heart pounding, I thought I understood why In a place which was being transformed before their very eyes into blackest night, the vanishing moon, which custom had convinced us was imperishable, was confirming by its gradual extinction the ancient belief that, whether the Indians were conscious of it or not, manifested itself in their every thought and action. What was happening now, they had known about since the very beginning of time. For them living had meant

nothing more than being crushed together in circumspect desolation, waiting for the one event worthy of the
name which was taking place this night, suddenly, once
and for all, without warning. The crowd was motionless.
Still and silent, they contemplated the darkness of the
sky which, as it increased, made the Indians' silhouettes
blacker and blacker until they vanished.

Meanwhile the moon was disappearing beneath
successive, ever more frequent waves of darkness.
Thick, recurring layers of shadow swept in again and
again from the outer edge until they gradually covered
the entire surface. At first you could still see the outline
of the circle, like a blue nimbus of derisory brightness; in
fact you could only call it 'bright' in contrast to the
absolute blackness against which it was silhouetted. But
at last even that faint trace was gone. There was no word
to describe the blackness that followed. And 'silence'
comes nowhere near describing that absence of life. I am
sure the dark entered as deep into them as it did into me,
removing any trace of that provisional, frail little light
which now and then they felt to shine within them. At
last we were seeing the true colours of our homeland,
free from the illusory and shallow variety conferred on
things by the fever that consumes us from the moment it
grows light and that does not cease until we have
plunged deep into the heart of night. At last we could
touch, from the outside, the soft, shapeless mass of the
void, which until then we had believed to be some absurd
notion of our own, the capricious invention of a spoiled
child in a world bound by need and innocence. After so
many presentiments, we were at last close to finding our
anonymous bed.

Coming as I did from the ports, where so many men
depend on the sky for survival, I knew this was an

eclipse. But knowing is not enough. True knowledge is recognizing that we know only that which condescends to reveal itself to us. Since that night I have always sought the shelter of cities. Though not out of fear. That night, when the blackness could grow no blacker, the moon little by little began to shine again. The Indians dispersed, returning to the village as silently as they had come, and went to bed almost satisfied. I remained alone on the beach. What came after that, what I call 'years' or 'my life', was the sound of seas and cities, the beating of human hearts, whose current, like an age-old river that washes away the useless paraphernalia of the visible, deposited me in this white room, to write, hesitantly, by the light of some almost spent candles, of a chance encounter that was both among yet with the stars.

Other Serpent's Tail titles of interest

Acknowledged as one of the great Latin American writers of the twentieth century, **Juan Carlos Onetti** was born in Montevideo, Uruguay in 1909. While working as a journalist in Buenos Aires, he was imprisoned under the military dictatorship in 1974 and on release, was exiled to Spain. His novels include his best known work, *The Shipyard*, and *Let the Wind Speak*. He was awarded Uruguay's national literature prize in 1963 and Spain's Cervantes Prize in 1980. He lived in Madrid until his death in 1994.

The Shipyard

'The Onetti experience is a curious one: readers end up feeling that they understand life better after a stay in this ghostly, tantalising world, only to lose the wisdom they have gained after a few hours of release from the spell. Combining the alienation of Camus with the fatalism of Eeyore... the form is subtle and delicate, the message sordid and bleak, the flavour inimitable' *Guardian*

'A totally three-dimensional exploration of the landscape of quiet despair' *Sunday Times*

'This literary landmark is here delivered in a wonderful translation that retains all the bleakness and poetry of the antihero Larsen as he attempts to salvage the unsalvageable' *Independent on Sunday*

'Onetti's vision is bleak but the pictures he conjures up against annihilation are vivid and beautiful' *The Times*

'In the literary vein of Camus... absorbing' *Morning Star*

'Considered by many to be Uruguay's finest writer… his eloquent brand of urban despair is so well turned that it remains vibrant and readable' Isabel Fonseca

'Is *The Shipyard* a one-off masterpiece? I hope that having reconstituted it for English readers, the translator and publisher will decide to take the rust off the rest of Onetti's works' *Spectator*

Let the Wind Speak

'Onetti's novels and stories are the foundation stones of our modernity. To those of us who are his followers, he brings a lesson of narrative intelligence and of immense love for the literary imagination' Carlos Fuentes

'Latin American literature has few secrets to divulge to the English-speaking world; but one of them is the Uruguayan novelist Juan Carlos Onetti' *Guardian*

'The Graham Greene of Uruguay… foreshadowing the work of Beckett and Camus' *Sunday Telegraph*

'Laconic, elegant, literary' *London Review of Books*

'A rare chance to catch up with the neglected Uruguayan novelist' *Metro*

'Onetti's world is sick and his hero sick of it, but his compelling, messy existentialism makes *Let the Wind Speak* a deceptively modern novel, and its reissue a cause for celebration' *Observer*

'I consider him one of the giants of the 20th century, certainly doing things in 1937/38 way before Beckett and Camus' Alan Warner

Juan Rulfo was born in Jalisco in Mexico in 1918 and died in 1986. He is the author of *The Burning Plain*, a collection of short stories and only one novel, *Pedro Páramo*. An anthropologist by profession, Rulfo is the great voice of the peasant condition.

Pedro Páramo

'*Pedro Páramo* is not only one of the masterpieces of twentieth-century world literature, but one of the most influential of the century's books; indeed it would be hard to overestimate its impact on literature in Spanish' Susan Sontag

'I like to think that Rulfo's moment in the English-speaking world has finally arrived. His novel's conception is of a simplicity and profundity worthy of Greek tragedy, though another way of conveying its unique effect might be to say that it is *Wuthering Heights* located in Mexico and written by Kafka' *Guardian*

'This brilliant Mexican novel, written in 1955, describes a man's search for his unknown father with the haunting clarity and strange logic of a recurrent nightmare' *Esquire*

Jorge Amado was born in northeastern Brazil in 1912. His early masterpiece is *The Violent Land*. A political exile in the 1940s, he lived for many years in Prague and Paris. The success of *Dona Flor and Her Two Husbands* brought Jorge Amado an international audience and translation into forty-six languages with more than eight million copies of his books in print. Jorge Amado died in 2001.

Dona Flor and Her Two Husbands

'A master storyteller… Jorge Amado has been writing immensely popular novels for fifty years. His books are on a grand scale, long, lavish, highly coloured… Amado has vigour, panache, raciness, exoticism' *TLS*

'A delightful read' *Financial Times*

'Not only has Amado brought to life the whole teeming city of Bahia where the story is set, but he has so filled it with musky perfume of physical love that it almost saturates the senses' *Cincinnati Enquirer*